THE SECRET OF SPIRIT MOUNTAIN

THE SECRET OF SPIRIT MOUNTAIN

Helen Kronberg Olson

Illustrated by Hameed Benjamin

DODD, MEAD & COMPANY
NEW YORK

F
0/s
c. 1

Author's note: Swalalahist—translated Indian Devils—was the actual name used in the area of the Northwest where this story has its setting.

1 2 3 4 5 6 7 8 9 10

Library of Congress Cataloging in Publication Data

Olson, Helen Kronberg.
    The secret of Spirit Mountain.

    SUMMARY: Tom is terrified when he is sent to
live with his grandfather, an Indian who reportedly
is hiding something awful on Spirit Mountain.
    [1. Indians of North America — Fiction.
2. Mystery and detective stories]
I. Benjamin, Hameed.   II. Title.
PZ7. 0519Se   [Fic]   80-1014
ISBN 0-396-07856-7

To my family

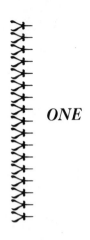

ONE

Tom reluctantly followed Mrs. Redding's sturdy figure up the two wooden steps and into the store. It took a few moments for his eyes to adjust from the winter sunlight to the darker interior. Mrs. Redding, seeming to have no such problem, marched up the narrow, box-stacked aisle to speak to the elderly woman clerk.

Feeling awkward standing by the door, Tom made his way to the counter. It was then the mingled smells of overripe bananas and stove oil hit him. Beads of perspiration broke out on his upper lip. In a wave of dizziness he clutched the counter, his hands finding room between a box of five-cent candies and a gallon jar of pickled prawns.

Mrs. Redding and the clerk didn't seem to notice. As if from far off, he heard the rise and fall of their voices. He shook his head to clear it. Why hadn't he had the courage to tell Mrs. Redding he'd rather stay in the car? But she made everything she said sound like a command. "You can't just sit there," she had stated. "You have to get out and get your circulation moving."

So now, even though his stomach was acting up, his circulation should be moving. Then why this numbness in his brain?

Tom shook his head again. Maybe this wasn't really he in this mountain town a million miles from nowhere. Maybe this was all a nightmare. Maybe in a few minutes his mother would call from the kitchen, "All kids sleeping in this house—up and out! Breakfast is ready."

The clerk's sharp laugh jolted his mind back to the present.

Mrs. Redding must have asked where Mr. Buche lived because the woman was exclaiming, "You really want to go up *there?*"

"That's what I said." Mrs. Redding's voice was firm.

"You sure couldn't get *me* to go up Spirit Mountain for all the money in the world," the woman said. "Do you know that old buzzard runs everyone off with a shotgun?"

Mrs. Redding snapped open her purse and extracted change. "For the two candy bars," she said. "And now would you mind just giving me the directions?"

But the woman had more to say. "That old man doesn't want visitors. They say he's hiding something up there." She glanced sidewise at them. "Something pretty awful."

Mrs. Redding's lips tightened. "Mr. Buche is this boy's grandfather. We can't have the child hear all these wild tales about the man before he even meets him."

The clerk now regarded Tom with interest. "What do you know," she said under her breath. "Who'd ever have thought he'd have a grandchild?"

Back in the Ford, rented hours before at the airport, Mrs. Redding gave an impatient shrug. "Don't pay any attention to that gossip about your grandfather," she admonished. "He couldn't be that rough or they'd have him in jail."

Tom chewed mechanically on a mouthful of candy bar. Everything was getting weirder and weirder, he thought. That this relative he was being dumped on was some kind of maniac just seemed to be more of the awfulness of the last two days.

Mrs. Redding pulled up at the town's only gas

pumps. "Better get it while we can," she said to Tom. To the man in oily coveralls who approached the car she said, "Fill it up. I hope there aren't any shortages up here."

"Plenty of gas up here," the man said. "Have to. We couldn't get out otherwise."

Tank filled, they crossed a bridge. And the town of Grindstone, with its post office, one general store, and combination gas station and garage, was left behind.

Now they climbed upward into the Cascade Range. Patches of snow began to appear beside the road. The farther up they went, the taller and darker the trees seemed to get. During the first few miles there had been an occasional building. Now there were none.

"See that one tree without leaves?" asked Mrs. Redding. "I think it's a maple. The tall ones, the evergreens, of course are firs. The Northwest is noted for its giant fir trees."

Right now, Tom thought, he'd like to see palm trees—Southern California palm trees. Was it only this morning he had been at home in Los Angeles? Only this morning he had talked to his mother in the intensive care ward at the hospital? Mom had looked so strange in all those bandages. They'd even shaved off her blonde curly hair.

Somehow that seemed the worst.

He felt the sting of tears. He turned his head so he could wipe his eyes with his jacket sleeve without Mrs. Redding's seeing him.

The oiled surface ended. The road continued, graveled and narrower. "We must be going to the end of nowhere," Mrs. Redding said. She seemed to be talking more to herself than to him. "Thank goodness they didn't have much snow up here this winter. We'd never have been able to make it."

"Hey, will you look at that!" Her foot jabbed the brake, causing Tom, who was taken unawares, to slide forward in the seat. "An old log house. And so huge. And way up here in the mountains."

Tom saw a two-story log house topped by several sagging chimneys. It was surrounded by a rail fence with many of its rails missing. A boy Tom thought to be about his own age was throwing a stick for a German shepherd dog to chase. As they slowed down, the boy straightened up to look at them. His eyes and Tom's met briefly. The boy waved. By that time Mrs. Redding had stepped on the gas again. It somehow seemed important to Tom that the boy should have seen him return the wave.

A mile after they passed the house, the road

11

ended as the store clerk had said it would. A dirt turnaround for cars led nowhere.

"A trail has to be here someplace." Mrs. Redding sounded annoyed. "Do you see it?"

Tom obediently peered into the dense tree shadows. "Isn't that a gate? Over there. That fence."

"See if it opens."

There wasn't much to the gate—a rusted fence length fastened to spikes on a tree. People weren't supposed to know a road was hidden behind it, Tom guessed. He waited until Mrs. Redding had driven the car through. Then he refastened the make-shift gate and got back into the front seat.

The trail, rocky and rutted and barely wide enough for a car, led steadily upward—up Spirit Mountain. There were no more remnants of civilization—no rusted fences, no fallen-down sheds—only boulders and forest going on and on across the mountains. Several snowcapped peaks rising from the range gave the scene an awesome grandeur.

"Beautiful, isn't it?" Mrs. Redding's voice cut shrilly above the sound of the laboring motor. "Well, isn't it?" she repeated when Tom didn't answer.

"Yes," he said. He had never been in any real mountains before. On film they had never looked this overwhelming.

Two deer startled by the car darted across the trail to disappear into the trees.

Were there other animals—more fearsome than deer—lurking in that dark forest? he wondered. Bears? Wolves? Cougars even?

Suddenly, like an unexpected bucket of ice-water thrown into his face, he remembered the "something pretty awful" the store clerk had said his grandfather was supposed to be hiding. In that shocked moment, the numbness that had kept him from thinking too much left him.

With fumbling fingers he rolled down the car window. Mouth open, he gulped the cold mountain air.

"Tom, you'll have to close that window. It's freezing in here."

No way could he stay up here, he thought as he rolled up the window. No way.

The woman edged the Ford around a rock slide. "From the condition of this road it looks as if we're the only ones who've used it in a long, long time." A frown creased her forehead. "I sure hope your grandfather is expecting you."

Maybe there was an out. Maybe his grandfather

hadn't received the Mailgram Mrs. Apple had sent to say he was coming. The man *was* miles and miles from a post office. Tom spoke for the first time that day, other than to answer the woman's questions. "Could I go back home if he doesn't want me?"

"No. He's your only relative, and you'll have to stay with him."

"Maybe Mrs. Apple will take me in."

"She has only one bedroom."

"I could sleep on the floor."

"No. She's already taking care of your little sister. That's enough for a woman of her age to handle." There was no mistaking the finality of her voice.

A deep canyon fell away on the right side of the steadily climbing trail. A stream which reminded Tom of a thin black snake could be seen winding far, far below. They bounced in and out of ruts, once coming too near the canyon's edge.

"If we get a flat tire we've had it," Mrs. Redding said grimly. "Someone should have warned me about this road. I would have thought your mother could have told me how it was going to be, even if she is in the hospital."

Tom only half heard her. It was starting again.

The nausea. "Nervous stomach," his mother called it.

When they came to a brief widening of the trail, he spoke. "Stop the car."

Mrs. Redding's head jerked toward him. "Why?"

He brushed the sun-streaked blond hair off his suddenly damp forehead. "I have to get out."

She stepped on the brake too abruptly. They were both flung forward.

Tom stumbled out of the car into a dirty patch of snow. Sharp, bare underbranches scratched his face as he pushed his way behind a tree trunk away from the woman's gaze. He rested his head against the rough bark while the airline's lunch and the candy bar came up.

Before he returned to the car, Tom mopped his face and shoes with Kleenex.

"You all right?"

He nodded.

"You ever ride in a plane before today?"

He shook his head.

"You probably have a delayed case of plane sickness." Mrs. Redding started the motor.

The trail left the canyon rim. The tall trees towered above them so thickly the branches meshed overhead. Mrs. Redding mumbled to herself as she switched on the headlights against the semidarkness. After that she didn't speak. Forehead knotted, she fought the wheel as the Ford bounced in and out of ruts.

Tom, now that his stomach felt better, searched his mind for an excuse to get him off this mountain and back home. Even if he had to stay alone in their house it would be a hundred times better than this place. Never would he stay up here. Ever.

"Finally." Mrs. Redding's voice echoed her relief. "There's the signboard the woman at the store said should be here."

Tom looked up. The message, faded and weatherbeaten, PRIVATE PROPERTY—KEEP OUT, could barely be read. It had been painted years ago. Hope rose in him. Maybe no one was here.

The car lurched out of the forest into a partly cleared area enclosed by a high wire fence. The fence was topped by two strands of barbed wire. Tom strained to see what was on the other side. No mistake, he thought. The area did look deserted.

Then, through a stand of trees, he saw it—a plume of smoke. Mr. Buche was home. . . .

Mrs. Redding stopped the car before the gate.

For a moment she didn't speak. She seemed to be considering what to do next. It came to Tom then that she might be worried about being shot.

"Open the gate," she said after a moment. "After all, you *are* his grandson."

The gate scraped the ground and then stopped. Tom tugged at it but it wouldn't budge.

"Lift it," she called.

He did as she told him, and it did move more easily. "Should I wait until you're through and close it again?"

"Hop in." Her voice held a new urgency.

Tom scrambled back into the car. She *was* afraid, he thought. She'd never leave him up here now. Why else had she wanted the gate open except to make a fast getaway? That was fine with him; he didn't want any closed gate standing in his way, either.

They drove slowly, cautiously around a straggling orchard, the dried remnants of a garden, a stand of tall fir, and clumps of rangy brush. At one point the noise of the car motor flushed out a lone goat from behind a mud-spattered jeep. The goat, bleating frantically, scampered away into the timber.

Mrs. Redding applied the brakes when the log cabin with its scattering of outbuildings came into

17

full view. "Get out," she said. "We want him to see we're harmless."

Tom reluctantly obeyed. He stood next to the car, holding onto its open door.

"Call," she directed fiercely. "Tell him who you are."

Tom opened his mouth. But no words came; he didn't know what to say.

She called then from the car window. "*Yoo-hoo,* Mr. Buche. I've brought your grandson—Tom." She waited for a few moments. Her voice grew shriller. "I'm a friend of your daughter-in-law. I've brought your grandson from Los Angeles."

No door opened. No face showed itself at any of the windows.

The goat bleated several times from its hiding place, the only sound in the mountain stillness.

Mrs. Redding called again.

Tom caught the movement from the corner of his eye. Out of the dense stand of brush, not ten feet from where he stood, a man emerged.

Tom felt his body go rigid.

An old Indian stood before them. He had flowing white hair, and his skin had the look of well-used leather. His deep-set eyes were shaded by a broad-brimmed black felt hat with a tall feather stuck into its beaded hatband. But to Tom the

18

most sinister-looking part of the man's appearance was a jagged scar which ran across his cheek to the point of his jaw.

The man stood steadily regarding the car. No one spoke or moved. After what seemed to Tom like hours, Mrs. Redding broke the silence. "Do you know where Mr. Buche is?"

The old Indian's mouth barely moved. "I'm Mr. Buche," he said.

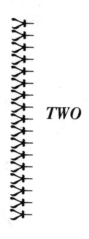

TWO

Tom braced himself against the car as he stared at the Indian who was his grandfather.

Mrs. Redding regained her composure almost immediately. She jerked open the car door and got out. Facing the man over the car roof, she asked, "Did you get the Mailgram?"

"No."

"Well, I should have known. The way this day's been going . . ." Her words flowed on, almost as if she were afraid to stop talking for even a moment in case she might not get started again. She explained about the car accident. That there was a possibility Tom's mother might never walk again. That she would be confined to therapy and rehabilitation after her injuries healed. That an elderly friend and neighbor, Mrs. Apple, was

20

caring for Tom's seven-year-old sister, Julie. That Tom needed a place to stay for an unknown length of time—perhaps years. That Mr. Buche was the only living relative—with the exception of Tom's father who hadn't cared enough about his wife and children to put in an appearance for the past five years or even to leave a forwarding address. That she, Mrs. Redding, worked with his daughter-in-law and had volunteered to bring Tom to Spirit Mountain. But it was important she catch a plane back to Los Angeles that very night.

While she talked, Tom's mind kept denying that this man could be his grandfather. Even though Julie and he had dark eyes, they had blond hair. How could they be related to this Indian?

Deep from some forgotten part of his brain came the answer. He remembered Mom had once said that, despite Tom's father's refusal to speak of his past, she wouldn't be surprised if his father was part Indian. But his own father had brown hair; Tom remembered that much. This fierce-featured man who stood before him looked all Indian.

"You don't know your son's address either?" Tom heard Mrs. Redding question sharply.

The man shook his head. "I've heard from my son's wife. Never from my son."

21

Tom knew well enough that his grandfather rarely answered his mother's letters. But whenever she had received a reply she'd posted the few paragraphs on their kitchen bulletin board so friends and neighbors could admire the precise handwriting. "From my husband's father," she would say proudly.

If only Mom knew, he thought. She, who was always planning trips north so they could visit the grandfather none of them had met. (Family was all important to Mom—probably, Tom guessed, because she had been an orphan.) If only Mom knew that this man—this Indian—who was supposed to be his grandfather hadn't looked directly at him, let alone spoken a word of welcome.

Well, he was glad—to him that meant only one thing. This relative, like his father, didn't want anything to do with him.

That was perfectly all right with him. He didn't want any part of this weird old Indian, either. Or this awful place. Anyone could see no kid could live up here. No electricity. No telephone. No nothing. Only mountains and trees going on and on forever.

Mrs. Redding spoke to him now. "Get your suitcase out of the back seat." She checked her wristwatch. "I have to go or I'll miss my plane."

Tom couldn't believe his ears. After she had seen all this, she still meant to leave him here! "I can't stay here." His voice tripped over the words. He thought desperately. "There isn't any school."

"Your grandfather will have to see that you get to school in town. It's the law."

Still Tom didn't move to open the door to the back seat. Neither did the man.

Mrs. Redding, looking exasperated, wrenched open the door herself, and, with Mr. Buche and Tom watching, pulled out an old blue suitcase. It hit the ground with a thump. She looked across at the man. "You know you are legally responsible," she said as if daring him to refuse. "You have to take him."

For the first time the old Indian looked at Tom. The eyes were black and expressionless.

Without realizing it, Tom shivered. Mom, who trusted everyone, might as well have thrown him into the panther's cage at the zoo, he thought.

The Indian spoke then, slowly, deliberately. "His father's Belgian mother would not let his father live here as a child. It would not be good for this boy either."

24

Tom cast a beseeching glance at Mrs. Redding. She *had* to take him back now.

But Mrs. Redding, who had been Mom's boss for many years at a downtown insurance office and whom Mom described as having a heart of gold under her tough exterior, acted as if the man hadn't even spoken.

" 'Bye, Tom," she said. "I'll let your mother know you arrived safely. Nice to have met you, Mr. Buche."

She clambered into the Ford as if she didn't have a moment longer to spare. She rolled up the window and then reached across to lock the doors. The vehicle jerked into motion.

Tom considered running after the car, begging her to take him with her. But he stood motionless. When he couldn't hear the motor's hum any more, he realized all hope was gone.

He looked up then and saw the man watching him, his face a mask, telling nothing.

Defeated, Tom went to the suitcase and picked it up.

"Come along," Mr. Buche said. He turned and walked toward the cabin. It was then Tom noticed that he had a slight limp.

Shoulders hunched, Tom followed the old

man, the heavy suitcase banging against his leg at every step.

When he hesitated at the door, Mr. Buche beckoned him to come inside.

The not unpleasant smell of wood smoke permeated the cabin. It reminded Tom of some place he'd been before but he couldn't quite remember where.

After his eyes had adjusted to the dim interior, his gaze wandered listlessly around what he supposed was the main room.

Small rugs of Indian design covered much of the bare wood floor. On the wall a pelt with black markings hung between several maps. Next to a large black stove with an outsize fire box stood a neat pile of wood.

The two bookcases seemed somehow wrong. The larger held row after row of large reference books. The smaller held an assortment of hardcover and paperback books. It seemed this old Indian read a lot.

It was then Tom saw the two guns. They hung from a rack next to the front door. "He runs off everyone with a shotgun," the store clerk had said.

Realizing he was staring at the guns, Tom turned his head to glance through an open bedroom door. Next to a bed covered with a red-and-black Indian blanket stood yet another bookcase.

His grandfather limped across the room to a second, closed door. He opened it. "You'll sleep in here," he said.

Tom's first impression, because of the musty odor, was that the room hadn't been in use for a long, long time. There was nothing Indian here. A patchwork quilt brightened the bed. Faded wallpaper with a design of toy trains decorated the walls.

"This was your father's room when he was a small boy," the old man explained gruffly. "For the short time he lived here."

Tom concentrated on one of the train's stubby engines. For him it would be a short time, too.

"You can put your clothes in there." Mr. Buche indicated an obviously handmade wardrobe cupboard. For a moment the old man stood looking at the cupboard as if he were seeing it for the first time. Abruptly he shook his head. Without another word he left the room, closing the door behind him.

Finally alone, Tom's built-up weariness asserted itself. He let the suitcase sag to the floor. With an effort he climbed onto the bed and spread himself flat. He lay there considering his situation. He would not unpack his suitcase, he resolved. He wanted to be ready to leave at a moment's notice.

His eyes traced the jagged yellow cracks on the papered ceiling. Had his father once looked at this same ceiling as he was doing now? he wondered. Had he had fearful thoughts of his Indian father? Or was he more afraid of whatever it was his Belgian mother had feared?

He would never know the truth, Tom decided. When his father used to drop in on his rare visits from his travels—bumming, he called it—he refused to give out any information about his own father. And Tom's Belgian grandmother had died before his own mother and father met.

A clock in the next room began striking. Five o'clock. That was the time his mother usually got home from work. In his mind he again saw his mother—head bandaged, eyes glazed—in the white room with the awful hospital smell.

Tom jerked to a sitting position and hit the pillow with all his might. The bedsprings pinged in protest. Fearful the old man had heard, he swung his feet off the bed and got up. He found his grandfather slicing carrots into a kettle.

"Supper time," said the man. "Get the water—outside at the pump." He pointed to a bucket on a small table.

Tom bit his lower lip. "I've never worked a pump," he admitted.

"Time you learned, city boy."

Stung by the words, Tom picked up the pail and went outside. The shadows were already lengthening. It would be dark soon. He would have to stay the night—that was for sure.

About eighty feet from the cabin stood the pump. Tom resolutely grabbed the handle and started pumping. Up and down. Up and down. *Creak, creak. Creak, creak.* No water came. Although the air was freezing cold, perspiration dampened his hands as he desperately worked the pump handle.

The water came. First grudgingly. Then in full flow. The bucket was filled to the brim before he stopped. Unheeded, water sloshed from the bucket to the ground as he made his way to the cabin. The city boy had conquered the pump, if nothing else, he thought without enthusiasm.

The man turned from poking a piece of wood into the stove.

Tom had barely set the bucket on its table when

he was handed a paring knife. "Peel the potatoes," directed his grandfather.

Tom had peeled vegetables for his mother more than once. But he had never been good at it. He took a potato from a wire basket. He was peeling the second one when he felt the old man watching him.

"No," Mr. Buche said. "You aren't doing it right. The peelings are too thick." He took the knife from Tom. While Tom stood there, biting his lower lip, the man quickly peeled the rest of the potatoes himself.

To Tom, the supper, with the exception of sourdough biscuits, was plain awful. Greasy fried potatoes, boiled carrots, and canned meat. He determinedly washed it down with a cup of bitter coffee, which was the only drink offered.

After supper, water was heated and the dishes washed. Tom dried. His grandfather couldn't criticize him about doing dishes, he thought. He was an expert in that department.

While Mr. Buche swept the floor, Tom leafed through a magazine. He found he was turning pages without really seeing what was on them. He closed the magazine and sat silently until his grandfather had finished. "I'd like to go to bed," he said then.

"We'll have to make it first." Drawers were opened and bedding removed.

Together they made the bed. Cotton blankets served as sheets. Two more quilts were added to the quilt on the bed. "That's it," the old man said, giving the pillow a shake.

As soon as his grandfather had closed the door, Tom undressed. The bed felt slightly damp, but it was soft. He blew out the lamp. But although he couldn't remember ever feeling so tired, his eyes stayed wide open. Thoughts of his grandfather, of his mother, of the father who had deserted them, of the store clerk's words, all ran around and around in his brain like small trapped animals.

It seemed like hours to Tom before the radio on the kitchen table fell silent. He heard his grandfather's footsteps enter the room next door. First one boot dropped to the floor, then the other. Bedsprings creaked as the old man got into bed.

Now, with the exception of the ticking of the wall clock in the kitchen and the sighing of the giant firs outside the window, all was quiet.

Still he did not feel sleepy. He decided it was too stuffy. His stomach contracted ominously. And then again. Nervous stomach? Or was it the greasy fried potatoes? Or both? Not now, he told himself. You just can't. But he knew there was nothing he could do to stop it. He was definitely going to be sick again.

The beginnings of heavy breathing punctuated by a snore drifted through the thin partition separating the bedrooms. His grandfather was asleep. Tom didn't know whether he was relieved or dismayed. All he knew was that his last chance to get a match to light the lamp was gone.

He pushed back the quilts and got up. By the faint light from the window he found his jacket in the wardrobe. Then he groped his way from the room.

He stood for a moment outside his grandfather's door. But every part of his being shrank from awakening the man. And what would he tell him? That he needed a light? That he had to get outside in a hurry? That he had a nervous stomach? "City boy," the old man would say scornfully.

He felt his way across the room. Twice he bumped hard against unseen furniture before he found the front door. Although he closed the door carefully behind him, it still emitted creaking noises.

Tall, black tree silhouettes hemmed in a patch

of sky lit by brilliant white stars. The night air, icy cold, chilled his body. But he could not stop. His supper left him about twenty feet from the cabin.

Afterward, exhausted, he sat on the frozen ground. His hands clasped around his knees, he looked up at the stars. A great longing for his mother came over him. For Julie. For his own bed in his own room at home. For the familiar sounds and smells of Los Angeles.

He pushed his way to his feet and went to the pump. Mechanically he worked the cold iron handle. When the water came he put his mouth to the spout.

"Hey, boy."

Tom jumped away from the pump so fast he tripped and sprawled on the ground.

Mr. Buche's dark figure towered against the sky. "What do you think you're doing out here in the middle of the night?"

Tom wiped his mouth with the back of his hand. "Drinking water," he mumbled.

The man's face remained in shadow. "Never come out here at night. Ever."

"Why?" Tom whispered.

The man turned away. "Some things are better

34

left unsaid." His white hair seeming to glow in the dark, he limped toward the cabin.

Tom stumbled to his feet. The store clerk had been right, he thought. He glanced over his shoulder at the dark forest. Shivering from more than the cold, he hurried after his grandfather.

THREE

The starting of a motor awakened Tom in the morning. Pale winter sun streamed through the window. How could he have slept so hard? he wondered. Last night when he went to bed he had been so sure he would never be able to sleep.

The floor was cold to his bare feet. Hurriedly he dressed. His grandfather wasn't in his bedroom. Nor was he in the kitchen. Since a fire crackled steadily in the stove, Tom figured the old man must have been up for some time. He went to the window and looked out. The jeep was gone.

A note lay on the table. "I am going up the mountain," the precise handwriting read. "Pancakes are in the warming oven. Coffee is in the pot. I'll be back by two o'clock. At noon open a can of beans and whatever else you find in the cupboard you want."

Tom's first reaction was one of relief. After last night he didn't much like to face his grandfather right away. Or ever, for that matter, he thought.

After he had eaten he put on his jacket and went outside. The tree branches and grass were tipped with frost. He looked around him. Why wasn't he permitted to go outside at night? he wondered. Since his grandfather had not said anything about daytime, he supposed it must be all right now. Still, he didn't feel like venturing far from the cabin.

He wandered aimlessly through the bare trees in the orchard and then back. A lean-to attached to the rear of the cabin claimed his attention. The unbidden question came: Could the "awful something" be hidden in the lean-to? Of course not, he assured himself. Casually he walked past the narrow door and then as casually walked back.

There was only one way to find out, he decided. He tried the knob. It gave easily enough. Through the open door he could see all of the small room. It was crammed with an assortment of things: machinery, shelves of canned goods, jars of fruit, sacks bulging with potatoes, apples,

37

and squash, dried corn and onions hanging from the ceiling, tools for carpentry, tools for auto maintainance, tools for gardening. There were many things stored in that room that a man living alone in the wilderness would need for survival— but there was nothing that looked suspicious.

The magazine on top of a stack in a corner looked as if it might be a *Popular Mechanics*. Leaving the door ajar, he went into the room. The light from the one small window was poor. He had to bend close to read. Before he knew it, he was immersed in an article.

The sudden slam jarred him back to the present. His heart beating overtime, Tom stared at the closed door. There was definitely someone or something on the other side. First there was a faint noise, followed by a sound like a snort. Scarcely daring to breathe, he listened. Then he heard the footsteps—leisurely, as if they had all the time there was. And they seemed to be walking away from the lean-to.

Tom crept to the window and peered out. A laugh caught in his throat. It was only the goat— the silly goat.

He left the building to call to the animal. She, for he could see it was a female, stopped to observe him. But she would not come closer. When he tried to get near enough to pet her, she shied away. Yet she didn't seem to be afraid of him. "All right for you now, goat," Tom said. "But we're going to be friends."

Near the lean-to stood the largest of the several sheds. Its north side was open. Cord wood sawed to one-foot lengths was stacked inside. On the dirt floor stood a large chopping block with an axe imbedded in it. Next to the block lay a few sticks of kindling.

Tom looked at the axe with interest. One of his neighbor's teenage sons had the job of chopping fireplace wood. Tom had often wanted to try his hand at it. Why not now? He could picture his grandfather's surprise at the big stack of kindling the city boy would have ready for him.

The axe wasn't all that easy to loosen from the block, he soon discovered. His grandfather, notwithstanding his age, must be very strong to bury it that deep. By working the blade back and forth, Tom was able to get it loose. He placed a piece of wood on the block and swung at it with all his might. In his mind he saw the wood split cleanly into two pieces. Something totally different happened. The axe jumped off the wood with a dull thud. The log flew through the air, barely missing the goat, which was standing at the opening peering inside.

Tom retrieved the wood and inspected it. "Dummy," he told himself. "This thing is full of knots." He sorted through the pile to find a knot-free piece.

He swung again. The wood split halfway through. He freed the blade and tried again. This time he was rewarded with two pieces of wood. "Got the hang of it," he told the goat, which had now come all the way into the shed.

He began splitting kindling with a will. Before he had a creditable stack of the stuff, he had to remove his jacket. Satisfied at last that he had chopped enough to surprise his grandfather, he put the axe down. "What else is there to do?" he asked the goat.

The goat ambled out of the shed and Tom, putting on his jacket, followed. She allowed him to walk next to her. But when he reached out his hand she jerked from his touch to run some distance away, where she stood regarding him.

"O.K. for you, goat," he said. He started to walk in the other direction. When he looked back he saw the goat, unperturbed, trotting toward the forest. He retraced his steps to follow her.

She had disappeared from sight when he got to the timber. A well-trodden path showed where she had gone. Tom brushed his hair off his forehead. He didn't much like entering the dark forest. If only the store clerk hadn't said all that weird stuff. "Goat, come back," he called.

No bleat answered his call. He took a few tentative steps up the path and stopped to listen. Running water. He was sure of it. Now his curiosity led him on.

It was a good-sized creek with ice clinging to its banks, the center flowing free. The goat, head bent, drank from a hole she had knocked in the thin ice.

"Hey," he told the goat, "it's big enough to swim in!"

The goat, now that she had drunk her fill, began eating grass near the water's edge.

A fish jumped not more than ten feet from Tom. Something inside him jumped, too. On the few times he had fished he had never even had a nibble, let alone caught a fish. And how he had tried. How he had cast and recast with the rented fishing gear. It came to him that his grandfather probably had fishing supplies. Of course he had, he assured himself. No doubt about it.

"Goat, I like you," he told the animal. She

41

looked up at him with a quizzical expression on her long face. This time she didn't resist when he petted her back. But she stood still only a minute before she was off to a new clump of grass.

Upstream another fish broke water. And then another. Tom sat down on a flat rock touched by the winter sun. The goat nibbled bark from a nearby branch. It seemed oddly peaceful. Things weren't all bad, Tom mused. A place to fish. And later, when it was warmer, a place to swim. Perhaps he would stay a couple of days. Just long enough for things to get better between his grandfather and himself.

True, the man wasn't at all the way his mother had imagined him to be. But at least he hadn't shot at them when they arrived. And he hadn't told them to leave. And maybe he was right about scolding him during the night. Maybe he had been afraid he'd get hurt outside in the dark. Maybe that's all it amounted to.

Feeling better, Tom got up, brushed the sand off the seat of his pants, and made his way back to the cabin. He just might come back here in the summer to visit. . . .

At twelve o'clock sharp he took a can of beans from the cupboard. He opened it and ate it all. Rummaging through the well-stocked shelves, he

42

found a pint jar of peaches. They were delicious.

With a sourdough biscuit spread with honey and an interesting-looking magazine, he curled up in a comfortable old-fashioned rocking chair. He rocked and munched and read. He could turn on the battery-powered radio if he wanted to, he thought. But he didn't.

His grandfather came home at one-thirty. Tom and the goat walked over to the jeep when it stopped. For some reason the man didn't look as strange to Tom today. Even the scar seemed to have lost much of its sinister cast. We're family, Tom reminded himself. I am his grandson.

"Hi, Grandfather." He got the name out quickly.

A flicker of surprise came and went on the man's face. "Hi." Mr. Buche hesitated only slightly before he added, "Tom." Favoring his game leg, he got stiffly out of the jeep. He reached back then, taking out a gun.

Tom recognized it as a rifle. Instinctively his stomach contracted.

The old man must have noted his reaction because he explained, "I thought I'd vary the menu tonight—venison." He reached into the jeep again and Tom saw he had a deer haunch half-wrapped in a white cloth.

43

His relief that his grandfather had used the rifle to hunt was so intense he didn't wonder until much later why there was only a venison haunch instead of a whole deer. Nor about the strange odor which clung to his grandfather's red mackinaw jacket.

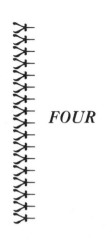

FOUR

"Today you go to school," Mr. Buche announced at breakfast.

Tom choked on a pancake. The evening before his grandfather had assured him, in answer to his questions, that he had all kinds of fishing gear, including hand-tied flies. To Tom's surprise, he had volunteered to teach him to fish scientifically. The boy had assumed that today he would receive his first fishing lesson. Instead here he was, going to school.

Dressed in his school clothes, slightly wrinkled from the suitcase, Tom climbed into the jeep next to his grandfather. A brown paper sack contained his lunch—venison sandwiches and two apples.

The ride down the mountain seemed to go much faster than when Mrs. Redding and he had driven up two days earlier. Tom had mixed feelings about the school idea. He conceded it would be nice to meet some kids his own age. And he was curious to see what a country school was like. But he did not intend to stay here, so what was the use of enrolling?

His grandfather surprised him further by stopping at the town's small store. "You have to get school supplies," he said.

Tom went with him readily. In all the awfulness of leaving home, he had not even packed a pencil.

When they entered the store, the woman clerk glanced up from marking prices on a box of canned goods. An expression of startled recognition flitted across her face when she saw Mr. Buche. She lowered her head abruptly to resume what she had been doing.

Tom picked out the bare necessities: a tablet, pen, and pencil. "Is this O.K.?" he asked. "Mom will send you the money."

"I am paying for anything you need. If you want anything else, get it."

"I guess this is all."

The woman wordlessly rang up the sale. She made change from the twenty dollar bill Tom's grandfather gave her, laid it on the counter, and then added a stiff, "Thank you."

Their next stop was the post office. Hope welled up in Tom. Maybe he would get a letter from Mrs. Apple telling him how his mother was. But there wasn't any letter. The postmaster said kindly, "Maybe next time, fellow."

His grandfather took no part in Tom's exchange with the postmaster. Instead he went directly to one of the larger mailboxes among the many that covered one wall and unlocked it with a key. The box was stuffed with newspapers and magazines—and the belated Mailgram from Mrs. Apple.

The school stood on a hill overlooking the town. When they arrived it was fifteen minutes before nine. Children of different ages played in the school yard. Mr. Buche led the way across the grounds to the main door.

There was always the same reaction, Tom noted, when the children looked up and saw his grandfather. Surprise—even fear. By the time they had walked halfway across the yard, all play had stopped and children were gathered in whispering clusters, watching their progress. Mr. Buche limped stolidly on, not paying any attention. Tom, by his side, tried to pretend indifference. But it was hard.

They went to the principal's office. The principal, on seeing Mr. Buche, looked as startled as the children. Hiding his surprise as best he could, he asked, "What can I do for you, sir?"

"My grandson, Tom Buche, will be going to this school."

"Your grandson?" The principal looked at Tom incredulously. Regaining his composure, he said, "Welcome to Grindstone School. I am sure you will enjoy it. Not overcrowded. Only four classrooms. Two grades to a teacher. Now, about your records. . . ."

School in Grindstone, Tom quickly decided, was much the same as in larger schools. Same lessons. Same rules. Same show-offs. At recess he made several friends—mostly, he suspected, because he caught a hard fly ball. Even though he was somewhat smaller than average, he had always been good at sports.

But it bothered him when the kids gathered around him to ask questions. Mostly about his grandfather. "Aren't you afraid of him?" was the most frequent one.

On the school bus that evening Tom sat on the long seat at the back. Charlie, a boy from his class that he'd instinctively liked, sat down on his right. Treena, Charlie's sister and a year younger, along with her friend Sue, also chose to sit at the rear of the bus. When Philip, the class loudmouth, attempted to squeeze in between the girls, there was much yelling and pushing.

"Quiet down back there," the bus driver called over his shoulder.

The girls reluctantly made room for a triumphant Philip. The bus rumbled into motion.

"Hey, man," Charlie said to Tom. "I guess Treena and I aren't the end-of-the-liners any more. Now you are."

It dawned on Tom that Charlie was the boy he'd waved to in the large log house when Mrs. Redding and he had driven by. They talked for a while before Tom asked, "Charlie, why do the kids think I should be afraid of my grandfather?"

Charlie cleared his throat. "Just crazy talk. Don't pay any attention to it."

"Tell him the truth," Philip yelled across Treena. "Tell him about the old 'devil man.' "

"Shut up, Philip," Treena said.

"He shoots at everybody who comes near his place," Philip persisted. "Everybody around here knows awful things are going on up Spirit Mountain."

Sue agreed. "I hate to admit it, but for once

squirrelly Philip is telling the truth. Even my dad heard horrible screams there just last spring. Philip's dad and some timber buyers were with him. As soon as it started to get dark, the screams began—human screams."

"Yeah," Philip said with relish. "My dad says old devil man is head of a bunch of screaming devils."

"Will everybody please shut up!" Treena said.

"That old devil—" Philip began, his voice loud enough to be heard throughout the bus. The other children were quick to turn around so they would not miss anything.

Charlie leaned toward Philip with a look of such fierceness that the younger boy stopped in midsentence. Then Charlie said to Tom, "You must have played a lot of ball to have such a good arm."

They talked about sports then, the girls chiming in. From there they went to life in the city compared to life in the mountains. Charlie and Treena had been born in Chicago.

But all the while they talked, Tom was thinking about what Philip had said about his grandfather. He had been there two nights and he hadn't heard any screams. And the old man, although he hadn't acted overjoyed to be stuck with a grandson, had acted decent enough—even offering scientific fishing lessons.

After Charlie and Treena got out of the bus, the driver took Tom the extra mile to the turnaround. " 'Bye, see you in the morning," the man called, his hand on the door control ready to yank it shut.

" 'Bye," Tom answered as he jumped off the last step.

The bus picked up speed and disappeared around a curve. Tom stood motionless in the shadow of the giant firs. What should he do now? Where was his grandfather? It came to him then that this might be the old man's way of getting rid of him.

The honk of a horn split the silence. For a moment Tom stood stock still. Then, jolted into action, he hurried to the make-shift wire gate.

On the other side, nearly hidden by brush, was the battered jeep.

"Right on time," said his grandfather.

"Right on time," Tom echoed the words. No matter what the kids said, his grandfather had been waiting for him.

In his relief he talked all the way to the cabin.

51

About school, at first. Then, not able to stop, he talked about Mom. And about Julie.

In the yard Mr. Buche stopped the car. But he sat there as if he didn't want to get out. As if he wanted to hear more.

Tom had had enough of talking. "Grandfather," he said. "If I split the kindling for you again, will you teach me how to fish when I finish?"

The old man reached for the door handle. "I will."

Tom caught three fish—one a whopping fourteen-inches long. Under his grandfather's instructions, he cleaned them himself. Fried in batter, they were the best fish Tom had ever eaten. Instead of coffee, he drank goat's milk. And to top off the meal was a dessert—corn pudding.

While Tom did his homework under the kerosene lamp, Mr. Buche sat nearby, the battery radio turned on softly. Tom glanced up once and caught his grandfather watching him. The black eyes did not look fierce at all.

He screwed up his courage to say, "I'm stuck with a problem. Could you help?"

His grandfather promptly bent his head to read where Tom pointed.

52

"You read without glasses," Tom said. "You must have good eyes."

"The best." The answer was followed by a clear explanation of how the problem should be solved.

As Tom watched his grandfather write on a scratch pad, he noted there were only a few black strands remaining in the coarse white hair. He wondered if he was very old. Without thinking, he put out his hand and touched the old man's arm. His grandfather looked up, and on his lips a smile half-formed.

The kids could say anything they wanted, Tom told himself later in bed, but his grandfather was a good person—he could tell. And besides that, he was smart, too. Tomorrow Tom decided he would write Mom a letter and tell her that his grandfather had taught him to fish, that he had helped him with his homework, that he, Tom, liked him. Imagining his mother's pleased smile, he went to sleep.

Later, his heart pounding in his chest, Tom awoke. He listened, scarcely daring to breathe. It came again—the most horrible-sounding scream he had ever heard. When it stopped, the silence was almost as awful as the scream.

Bedsprings squeaked in the next room. Then

the sounds of getting up, of getting dressed. Another scream ripped through the night, fading away to stillness.

A flicker of a flashlight's beam crept through the open door into Tom's bedroom. He held himself rigid, pretending sleep. His grandfather's footsteps moved softly away.

After the outside door closed, Tom realized he hadn't heard the old man take the gun from the wall rack. That meant his grandfather knew all about what was going on outside.

Now a crescendo of agonized screaming rent the air.

Tom sat up, his hands on his clothes. He wanted to be ready.

But, as abruptly as they started, the screams stopped.

When time passed and the screams did not resume, the boy's hands began to relax. A sound by the front door caused his fingers to tighten their grip on his clothes.

Limping footsteps. They could only belong to his grandfather. Tom slid down under the covers. When the old man paused at his door, he pretended he was asleep. It was then Tom became aware of the strange scent which seemed to cling to his grandfather's clothing.

Ears alert, Tom listened as the man walked away to go into his own room. The springs squeaked several times. Soon heavy, even breathing told him his grandfather slept. But it was a long time until he, himself, could relax—let alone sleep.

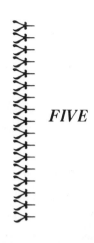

FIVE

Tom did write the letter to his mother. But he barely mentioned his grandfather. And he didn't mention the screams at all. Never would he let her know about them.

Now that he had heard those screams he wanted to go home more than ever. Night after night, waiting for the screams and fighting "nervous stomach," he would resolve that first thing in the morning he would tell his grandfather he had to leave. In his mind he would phrase the reasons in different ways.

But in the morning light he found he couldn't bring it up. Mostly because of his mother. He was now receiving regular letters from her. She was getting better, but she always closed each letter with the sentence: "I am thankful every day

57

you are with your grandfather and I know you are well cared for."

Weeks passed. And, since there were no more screams, he began to relax. He also found that, in spite of the mystery surrounding his grandfather, his respect for the old man grew steadily.

School, too, was O.K. And the kids, now that they were satisfied he was as average as themselves, rarely referred to his grandfather. Charlie and he really hit it off. Tom felt good that Charlie, the most popular boy in school, had chosen him to be his best friend.

With his life running fairly smoothly, the cabin on Spirit Mountain began to feel more like home—or at least more like his home away from home.

And then one dark night it happened again.

The screams, when they awakened him, seemed even more scary than he remembered. As he had the first time, he pretended sleep while his grandfather got up, dressed, and went outside. A few minutes later, the screaming stopped. Yet his grandfather didn't return for at least an hour.

Tom's relief that whatever had been outside was gone and he was safe was short lived. Now all he felt was anger—anger at his grandfather. "He should have known all that racket would have waked me," he muttered. "He didn't care enough about me to stay inside." It angered him further that soon the old man slept peacefully as if he had not a worry in the world. Mind churning with resentment, he, himself, wasn't able to get back to sleep until it was almost time to get up.

The next noon he sat, hands clasped around his knees, under an oak in a far corner of the school ground.

Charlie found him there and flopped down beside him. "What's eating you, man? As soon as I got on the bus this morning I noticed that funny look on your face."

Tom studied his knees while he considered if he dared tell what had happened last night.

"Charlie," he started. "You know what Philip and Sue said the first day on the bus? About awful screams on Spirit Mountain?"

Charlie looked off into the distance. "Yeah . . ."

"Well, what would you say if I told you—"

Brrrrr. The strident clamor of the school buzzer shattered the air.

Noon hour was over. Play groups dissolved as children ran for the building. Tom automatically scrambled to his feet.

Charlie leaped up beside him. "Told me what? Come on, spill it."

Tom shook his head. Then he turned and sprinted after the others.

Charlie ran to catch up with him, but Tom was able to outrun his friend.

"Hey, man," Charlie whispered in the hall. "You're some runner."

In the evening they sat on their regular seats at the back of the bus. Tom was relieved that Charlie did not question him further. He was relieved, too, that the buzzer had interrupted him. He had almost spilled it, he thought. And no matter what awful thing his grandfather was mixed up in, he would protect him. He would never tell anyone—not even Charlie. He owed his grandfather that much.

Although Philip and Sue and Treena were engaged in their usual noisy conversation, Tom did not take part. Charlie, beside him, was quiet, too.

A few minutes before they came to the old log house with its broken rail fence, Charlie asked, "Hey, Tom, would you like me to stay over with you one night?"

Tom, caught unawares, searched for an excuse. "There isn't any extra bed," he said finally.

60

"Hey, we have sleeping bags. I could bring up two, and we could sleep out for the night. How's about it?"

Tom shuddered involuntarily. "No."

Charlie gave him a measuring glance, and then shrugged his shoulders.

The bus rolled to a stop. Tom nudged Charlie's arm. "Thanks."

Charlie swung himself into the aisle. "Remember, I'm your friend."

Treena stood up to follow her brother. "Me, too," she said. "I'm your friend, too."

Tom had gotten into the habit of going up to sit behind Mr. Clinton, the bus driver, and talking with him the last mile of graveled road. This evening he did not move from his seat.

The bus ground to a halt. "End of the line," Mr. Clinton called.

Tom got off slowly. The bus had disappeared around the curve before he started for the makeshift gate. Absently kicking at stones, he made his way to the battered jeep.

"How was school today?" His grandfather asked his usual question.

Other nights there was much to tell. Tonight he merely answered, "O.K."

The motor coughed, and the jeep began its jolting ascent of the mountain. Tom stared into the canyon. The river looked as if it were drawn with a black crayon, he thought. Aloud he said, "Why did my grandmother take my father away from here when he was small?"

As if he hadn't heard, the old man continued to look straight ahead.

"Why?" Tom asked.

The face did not change expression, but now the words emerged. "Since you are of my flesh and blood I suppose you have a right to know." He drew a deep breath and then expelled it. "I will start at the beginning. She was from Brussels—a big city. I met her in Belgium—World War I. I was billeted in her family's home. They spoke French. So did I—I had learned it from my father. He was half French, you know."

Tom hadn't known. There would be a time when he would want to learn more about his great-grandfather, but not right now. "What happened then?"

"We learned to love each other." The gruff voice softened. "We were married."

He slowed the jeep to let a squawking pheasant clear the road. "It was wrong and I knew it. But when you are young—we were both eighteen—

you are impetuous. Soon after, I was injured. My leg, and"—his hand went to the scar on his face and then dropped back to the steering wheel—"a couple of other places.

"The war ended. For many years I lived and worked in Belgium. My young wife thought all was well. But I knew it couldn't last. I knew someday I would have to go home." He took another deep breath and expelled it. "To take over the trust."

Tom glanced sideways at his grandfather. What did he mean by "the trust"? he wondered.

But the old man did not explain. "First I received word my mother had died. And then— within months—my father. I had waited too long. I was the only one left—the last of our tribe. I had to return immediately.

"She—my wife—had never seen wild country like this before. But she was willing. So I was happy. I was home—on Spirit Mountain. And— very important to me—at last a son was born to carry on—to take over the tribe's trust when I, in my turn, would die. . . ." His voice trailed away.

"The trust of what?"

His grandfather applied the brake and slowed the car until it was barely running. Now his intense black eyes studied Tom. "You must promise to tell no one," he said.

"I promise."

"The Swalalahist—the trust of the Swalalahist."

Tom felt his grandfather's gaze boring into him, waiting for his reaction. He repeated the Indian-sounding name to himself, but it remained just a word. "What happened then?" he asked.

His grandfather pressed his foot down on the gas pedal. "She began asking questions. It was then I presumed too much. In my stupidity, I had her meet them—the Swalalahist." His shoulders hunched. "It was a mistake. She would not stay another day. She took our tiny son and left." He paused a moment before he added, "I did not see her again—or my son."

The Indian word now had meaning—terror. "The Swalalahist," Tom asked. "Will I see them?"

"No." The answer came slowly. "I don't want you to go away, too."

Tom stole a glance at his grandfather's profile. Then he saw it—a lone tear tracing its way down the jagged scar's path.

The Swalalahist were forgotten. Love for his grandfather welled up in him. His only thought

64

was to reassure him—to take away his hurt. "Grandfather," he said. "I won't leave—I promise."

"Blood of my blood," the old man murmured. "Flesh of my flesh." His smile reminded Tom somehow of the sweet, surprised smile of Julie when he had met her accidentally in the school hall one day.

They rode the rest of the way to the cabin in silence. At the gate Tom started to get out. His grandfather laid a staying hand on his arm. "I have been fearful these many years that there would be no one to carry on the trust. But now . . ."

Tom gently pulled his arm free. He didn't want to hear about the trust. He jumped out of the jeep and unlatched the gate.

When his grandfather had driven through, Tom waved him on. "I feel like walking," he said. Tilly, the goat, nuzzled his hand in greeting. Out of habit, he stroked her head, and together they walked toward the cabin. Why had he promised to stay? He loved his grandfather, he knew that now. And his grandfather obviously loved him. That was for real. But the Swalalahist. . . ? His young grandmother had fled at the sight of them. Tom shivered. The screams in the night were awful enough. Even if he was grandfather's flesh and blood, he didn't want the trust of the Swala-lahist—he shivered again—ever.

His grandfather had already started supper. He looked up when Tom entered the room. "We're having my specialty." The old man spoke in a more joyful tone than Tom had ever heard before. "Hunter's stew."

He's happy because he thinks I'll take over the trust, Tom thought miserably. He asked aloud, "Can I help?"

"Yep. Since you're a rotten potato peeler, how about tackling the carrots? You scrape them."

While the stew simmered, the old man mixed up a batch of sourdough biscuits. Good smells filled the kitchen.

Tom ate two helpings.

After supper his grandfather brought out a checkerboard. "All work and no play makes for bored and boring people," he said.

Tom was quickly beaten in three games. The old man shook his head. "It's high time I taught you the finer points of checkers." Moves were analyzed. Tom found he was playing a better game.

When the checkerboard put away, his mind, like a magnet, fastened on the Swalalahist.

"Let's not go to bed right away," he suggested. "Let's listen to the radio."

The old man glanced at the wall clock. "It's late. Your mother wouldn't think I was taking good care of you if she knew I was letting you stay up this long."

"Let's see what the weather will be," Tom said, relying on his grandfather's fondness for weather reports.

"All right, young fellow. Just until then. That should be in about ten minutes."

Tom cupped his hands in his chin and tried to appear wide awake.

The news came first. Mr. Buche listened intently until the report was ended. He shook his head. "When will those in power ever learn," he said, "that it is their duty to protect, not destroy?"

The weather was next: "Freezing during the night in the Cascades. Down to ten degrees."

"I'll be glad when I see spring," the old man mused. "Time for planting." He reached for the radio's off knob.

The scream—horrifying in its suddenness—cut through the room.

Tom's head jerked out of his hands. His gaze flew to his grandfather.

The old man froze in midsentence. But only for a moment. Deliberately he turned off the radio. Then he arose and went to the peg upon which his red jacket hung. When he had put on the heavy mackinaw, he turned to Tom. "I'll be back later. You go to bed."

"The Swalalahist?" Tom whispered.

He nodded. "Now go to bed like I told you." He bent and picked up the flashlight and left the cabin, closing the door firmly behind him.

Tom sat where he was, not sure whether he should obey his grandfather. A scream farther off was echoed by one near the gate. Then several came at the same time. Biting his lower lip to keep it from trembling, Tom decided it would be wise to blow out the lamp and get into his bedroom.

Dressed, except for his shoes, he lay in bed, body taut, listening. But there were no more screams. Why? he wondered. Could they be pets? The thought came to him then that he had never heard a cougar. Maybe this awful screaming belonged to cougars. His grandmother, a city woman, would have been plenty frightened of cougars, he reasoned.

Feeling better, he drifted into sleep. But when his grandfather returned he awoke. He got up on one elbow. "Grandfather," he called. "Are the Swalalahist cougar?"

"Cougar?" the old man repeated. "No. Whatever gave you that idea?"

Tom felt the familiar sick feeling clutch his stomach. He had been so hopeful they were cougar. What were they, then? Part of his mind shrank from knowing, and yet he couldn't let it rest. "What does Swalalahist mean in English?" he asked.

His grandfather didn't hesitate. "Indian devils," he said. "Swalalahist means Indian devils."

Tom tried to speak but all that came out was a croak. He tried again. "Grandfather—I don't—think—I should stay after all. I think I should go—home."

SIX

The light streaming onto his bed awakened Tom. He glanced at his wristwatch. The sun was coming up earlier. He would be glad when spring came and it would be warm enough to swim.

He remembered then. He would not be here for spring. Last night he had told his grandfather he wanted to leave—right away.

He thought of his grandfather. Only yesterday the old man had joyfully made stew for him. Had taught him to play a better game of checkers. Had shed a tear because he didn't want his grandson to leave—like the others.

Tom threw back the covers in disgust. "Tom Rat Buche," he said to himself. "What makes you such a big coward? One minute you promise your grandfather you'll never leave him, and the next

70

you hear the English name for Swalalahist and you go into a panic."

"Indian devils, Indian devils." The words, unbidden, whispered through his brain.

He flopped back onto the bed. Where could he go, anyway? To Mrs. Apple's? Hardly. Mrs. Redding's? Never. He considered his friends' homes, one after the other. None of them had room for an extra person. If only he could live at home.

He sat up. Maybe there was a way. Why hadn't he thought of it before?

His mother had mentioned in her last letter that she was progressing much faster than the doctors had anticipated. That she was able to stand and even take a few steps. "If only," she had written, "I could stay at home and go to the rehabilitation hospital as an outpatient. But that's wishful thinking. I know it's impossible."

He would write a letter to her today. Tell her he was able to care for her. He had learned from his grandfather how to cook, at least enough to get along. And he had learned other things—lots of other things. He imagined his mother's surprise and joy when she received the letter.

Feeling as if pieces of a jigsaw puzzle had clicked neatly into place, he swung his legs over

71

the side of the bed. He could face his grandfather now. He had a good excuse—and it wasn't as if he intended to leave right this minute, either.

His grandfather acknowledged his good morning with a subdued nod.

"I am sorry about last night," Tom said as soon as they sat down for breakfast.

The old man shook his head. "I am the one to be sorry. I should not have told you about the Swalalahist. You are too young to be burdened with such knowledge."

"But I wanted to know." Tom looked him full in the face. "I heard them screaming twice before last night."

His grandfather lowered his head to stare into his coffee cup. "I should not have let you stay. I should have protected you from all this. Forgive me. An old man's loneliness overcame reason."

Quick pity tightened Tom's chest. But he had to say it. "The way I figure it, Mom could come home if someone took care of her. I could. You taught me how to cook—and other things. But it wouldn't be right away. She'd have to get permission from the doctors and stuff like that." The words were out. He waited.

"Whatever you wish."

Tom drew a relieved breath. The hard part

was over. He had told his grandfather he wouldn't be staying. And without anything further being said, his grandfather knew that he, Tom, wasn't taking over any tribal trust—ever.

Now that he was on safe ground he could ask questions—find out things. "Tell me about the Indian dev—" he caught himself—"about the Swalalahist."

His grandfather pushed back his chair. "I have told you too much already. I only hope you forget what you already know."

"But, Grandfather . . ."

"I don't want to talk about it." Tom saw that the fierce expression of the first day had reclaimed the old man's face. He knew he dared not question further.

At school that noon he went directly to the isolated oak tree. He sat, his back against the cold bark, mulling over what he had learned about the Swalalahist. Few answers. Mostly questions.

"Hey!" Charlie stood over him. "You're supposed to pitch. What gives, man?"

Tom looked up. "Your father was born here, wasn't he?"

Charlie dropped his mouth in an exaggerated

expression of surprise. "What does that have to do with baseball?"

"All I want is an answer."

"Yeah, he was born here. So was my grandmother. So was my great-grandfather. I wasn't though. Sorry."

"Your great-grandfather was born here? Hey, that's neat. Could I talk to him sometime?"

"Sure, why not?" Charlie grabbed Tom's arm and hoisted him to his feet. "Let's get going. You're holding things up."

Together they ran across the grounds to the ball diamond. Sue called from the plate, "Hurry it up. I'm first batter, you know."

Tom whirled to face Charlie. "When can I talk to him?"

"Why don't you stay over tonight?"

"How about tomorrow night? That is, if your parents and my grandfather say it's O.K."

His grandfather showed no surprise when asked for permission. "Whatever you want to do."

Tom had met Charlie's parents previously. When he entered the huge, rundown log house, they greeted him warmly. Charlie introduced him to the little wisp of a man Tom had seen several times puttering around the yard. "My great-

74

grandfather, Mr. Egan, better known as Gramps.''

"Ninety-eight years old," Mr. Egan told Tom proudly.

Charlie's grandmother laid aside her knitting to shake hands. Tom noted that she, Mr. Egan, and Charlie's father had a strong resemblance to each other. Treena had told him as they came up the walk from the bus that they had moved from Chicago because their grandmother needed help. After their grandfather had died suddenly, it was difficult for her to handle the family's timber interests alone. "None of us was crazy about coming here except Daddy," she said. "But now none of us would ever go back."

Tom was glad they had stayed. He found he enjoyed the evening meal a lot. The food was simple but good. Most of all he enjoyed the give and take of family conversation which he had missed. Several times during the meal he thought of his grandfather's self-imposed isolation from people. Surely the old man could have stopped every so often to visit Mr. Egan, his nearest neighbor.

After they had eaten and the dishes were cleared from the table, a vote was taken on what program to watch on the battery-powered television set. An undersea-life documentary won out.

Tom sat down next to Mr. Egan on the davenport. Treena plopped down on the other side of Tom. She immediately began a conversation. "Tom, I am going to interview you. All in the interests of science, you know. Do you like blonde, brunette—or redheaded girls the best?"

Tom, who had been informed by Sue many times that Treena was "mad for him," looked at Treena's red hair and grinned. "All in the interests of science, the answer is all three."

"You're hedging," Treena said. "I want a straight answer."

Charlie interrupted. "Tom doesn't want you asking him dumb questions. He wants to talk to Gramps about old times up here."

"Really?" She looked at Tom.

"If you don't mind we could get back to our interview later. By then I could probably come up with some super scientific answers."

She got up. "I'm expecting you to keep your word, Mr. Tom Buche."

Tom grinned at her before he turned to Mr. Egan.

"Do you really want to know about old times?" Mr. Egan asked.

"Yes, I do."

76

The old man looked pleased. "Well, you've come to the right person."

"I wanted to find out about the tribe of Indians that lived on Spirit Mountain—especially about my grandparents."

The faded blue eyes scrutinized Tom with interest. "Say, you're sure a light-headed Indian kid."

Something deep inside Tom expanded with pride. He liked being called "Indian kid." His shoulders straightened and he sat a little taller. "My grandfather's mother was all Indian."

"She sure was. Dressed like an Indian. Spoke only Indian, too, as far as I ever knew. Her husband was half Indian and half French. His father was a French fur trader. The traders mostly married Indian women."

"Did you know my grandfather when he was a boy?"

"Of course I knew who he was, but he kept to himself even then. He didn't go to school here. He went off to some Indian school."

Tom decided it was time to ask. "Why do people call my grandfather a devil man?"

Mr. Egan didn't look surprised. He seemed to sense that this question was the reason for the

conversation. "I don't know if it's my right," he said.

"I must know."

Mr. Egan rummaged in his pocket and brought out a rumpled paper sack. He held it toward Tom. "Have a peppermint."

Tom peered inside the sack before he reached for one of the round white candies.

Mr. Egan placed a peppermint in his own mouth. "Some of it's tales, I expect, but . . ." He paused, his eyes taking on a faraway look.

"Please tell me."

"Well, I don't think anyone knows any more than I do. The Indians of Spirit Mountain are all gone—'cepting your grandfather. And all the original settlers are long dead, too."

Tom nodded.

"There were many strange stories about Spirit Mountain. Some of the trappers who happened to stray onto the tribe's land said the Indians up there could take on the shape of terrible-looking monsters to scare the people away. Heard stories about those Indians eating people, too." He held out the sack. "Have another peppermint."

Tom shook his head.

Mr. Egan placed a peppermint on his tongue.

79

He savored it a moment before he continued. "Of course the white people got scared silly. Every time they'd see an Indian they'd be afraid for their lives. I heard it finally got so bad that any time anything happened to anyone—a fire or an accident—they'd blame it on the Indians of Spirit Mountain.

"Then a retired army man moved out here. He got the people of the territory so inflamed against the tribe that the men banded together into an army. Then they invited all the men of the Indian tribe to come to a peace meeting— about fifty miles from here.

"That's where they bushwhacked the Indians. What was left were forced to leave and go onto reservations in the southern part of the territory. Many died on the way and many died on the reservations." He shook his head. "Awful, wasn't it? The only Indian family allowed to remain on the mountain was your grandfather's family—because your—let's see—great, great-grandfather was French." The old man paused. It was then Tom became aware that his stomach didn't feel right.

Mr. Egan began again. "But the trappers still claimed they saw the Indian devils up there—in more monstrous shapes than ever. And that's the

80

way it remains. That's why your grandfather is known as the devil man. People in these parts are convinced there are Indian devils on Spirit Mountain. Not one of them dares go up there." He scratched his head. " 'Cept timber buyers who want to get their hands on that virgin forest. Your grandfather runs them all off with a gun."

"Do *you* believe there are Indian devils?"

Mr. Egan gave Tom a level look. "There's something awful up there. I knew one old trapper who saw the Indian devils very well."

"What did he say they looked like?"

"Funny thing. Old George said they were too horrible to describe. He didn't want to talk about it. Later he lost his mind completely."

Tom knew for certain he was going to be sick, but he had one more question. "Do you know the Indian name for those devils?"

Mr. Egan gave a short laugh. "Probably I'm the only one around who does. An old witch of a woman used to warn us when we were kids, 'If you aren't good, the Swalalahist will come at night and snatch you out of your beds, and your parents will never see you again.' "

Tom knew he dared not wait a moment longer. "Where's the bathroom?" he asked.

SEVEN

When his grandfather picked him up at the turn-around the next afternoon, Tom was relieved to see that he was smiling. Obviously the old man was trying to resume their former relationship.

"Did you have a nice visit?" he asked.

"Yes, very nice."

"Tilly missed you. She kept looking for you."

Tom could only nod, while a perverse small voice inside him wondered if the goat was an Indian devil changed shape.

"Did you receive another letter from your mother?"

"No—I expect I'll hear from her tomorrow, though." He sure hoped he would. He wanted to hear she thought his plan a good one.

At the cabin Tilly seemed determined to enter

the door with him. He stooped to pet her. "Good old Tilly," he said. "So you missed me, you funny old goat." He firmly pushed her outside and closed the door on her doleful bleating. Tilly was just a goat, and his grandfather was just his grandfather, so why did he feel so strange? His gaze lingered on the animal pelt nailed to the wall. He couldn't help wondering what awful things the animal had seen before he became a decoration. He shook himself. "I'm going out to split wood," he said.

When he returned to the cabin he found his grandfather had outdone himself cooking supper. He had fixed things Tom especially liked. He had even baked a wild huckleberry pie from the berries put up the previous fall.

Tom ate more to please his grandfather than because of appetite. Yet, though they kept up a polite conversation, everything he and his grandfather said sounded stiff and unnatural to his ears.

After the dishes were washed and put away, Mr. Buche brought out the checkerboard. "How about a few quick games before you tackle your homework?"

Tom hesitated. "I'm sorry, Grandfather," he said. "I have too much to do tonight."

"Of course. Homework comes first."

"I have to read this book—and make a report."

"Of course. I have a book from the state library I've been waiting to get into, too."

Tom opened the book. Self-consciously he read two pages. He glanced up to find his grandfather looking at him. They both dropped their eyes to their books.

Tom read another page and stood up. "I think I'll go to my room and read lying on my bed."

"Good idea—it's more comfortable that way."

For the first time since he'd come to Spirit Mountain, Tom closed his bedroom door himself.

Away from his grandfather's gaze, he tried to get interested in the book. Failing, he undressed and went to bed. After he had blown out the lamp on the nightstand, he lay back on the pillow. The wind had begun to blow, he noticed. He remembered having heard the radio weather-caster say there might be winter thunderstorms in the mountains.

Resolutely he closed his eyes. Yet, because his ears kept straining to hear over the wind, he could not sleep. Sometimes he was sure he heard faint screaming far away in the mountains. He would listen. But even when he knew for certain it was only the wailing of the wind, he could not relax.

His hand found the matchbox on the nightstand and he relit the lamp. The toy trains running up and down the wallpaper somehow made the thought of screaming devils seem unreal. After a while he blew out the lamp. Even though the wind had picked up strength, he dozed off.

The sharp sound of something breaking near the cabin awoke him with a start. Hurriedly he sat up. Within moments he heard his grandfather putting on his clothes. The doorknob of his bedroom turned, and a flashlight's beam swept the room. His grandfather spoke: "Thought you'd be awake. It seems as if the wind broke a limb. I'm going to see if Tilly's all right."

"Leave my bedroom door open, please."

"Sure." When the outside door was opened a gust of wind rushed through the cabin.

Tom stayed sitting up. Only the wind, he mused. He had been prepared for something worse. Pale lightning lit the room, to be followed somewhat later by muted thunder.

His grandfather returned. "Branch just missed the roof," he said. "Going to be a nasty thunderstorm." The flashlight's beam disappeared as he went inside his own room. "Good night, Tom," he called through the partition. "Better get some sleep."

"Good night," Tom murmured in a voice too

low to be heard. But he continued to sit up.

In a few minutes his grandfather's breathing told Tom he slept. Now the boy felt regret he hadn't answered louder. Springs creaked as his grandfather shifted in his sleep. Unaccountably, the old man sighed.

The sigh sounded to Tom awfully sad—like the sigh of a man who had no friends—no relatives, even. He scooted down under the covers. Tomorrow he would be very nice to his grandfather.

The wind changed, blew from the east. A fierce gust rattled the windows. A succession of gusts followed, each stronger than the last.

Over the sound of the wind another sound emerged—the frantic bleating of Tilly.

Tom sat up again. His grandfather, undisturbed, slept on.

The goat's bleating became more intense. Tom moved to the side of the bed and looked out the window. Lightning flashed so rapidly it temporarily blinded him. Thunder rolled up and down the mountains. He wished his grandfather would awaken.

A swath of sheet lightning lit up the yard as brightly as day. In the split second of illumination, Tom saw a line of movement at the edge of the forest. Had he imagined it? he wondered. Breath held, he waited for the next flash of light. This time there was no mistake. A dark mass was headed directly for the cabin.

In his haste to get out of bed, the cotton blankets became tangled around his body. He took them with him as he half-walked and half-fell, getting to his grandfather's room.

"Wake up," he whispered through chattering teeth. He shook the old man's arm. "Please. Please."

"What is it?" his grandfather asked as he struggled to a sitting position.

"They're coming here!"

His grandfather switched on his flashlight. "So," he said, his voice calm. "So. It must be a bad storm. That brings them."

"I'm afraid they will break in—" Tom was going to add— "and eat us," but he caught himself. Instead his trembling increased.

His grandfather put his arm around him. "Do not be afraid," he said gently.

There was a sudden lull between thunderclaps. Tom heard it then. A low, monotonous rising and falling of voices. "They're chanting," he whispered. "They're right outside the cabin chanting. What are we going to do?"

Lightning so bright it seemed to dissolve the walls came and went. His grandfather's answer was buried in the instant boom of thunder.

The storm's first hailstones tripped across the roof. Immediately an ear-shattering deluge of hail pounded the cabin.

Then came a brief cessation. A ragged scream filled in the interval, the terrible anguish of the cry echoing in the room.

"I must go outside," the old man said.

"No. They might kill you."

"We are brothers." Determinedly Mr. Buche loosened himself from Tom's clasp. Within minutes he had slipped on his clothes. Then, taking the flashlight with him, he left the house.

"*Yahoo,*" Tom heard his grandfather call in the yard.

The chanting ceased. Then Tom heard his grandfather speaking in a language he couldn't understand. Although the old man was shouting because the storm's noise had resumed, there was no mistaking the concern in his voice.

He really does believe they are his brothers, Tom thought. With rising panic he dove into his grandfather's bed and pulled the covers over his head. If the old man should trust them enough to bring them into the cabin, *he* didn't want to see them—or worse, have them see him. If a tough old trapper couldn't take the sight of them without losing his mind, how could he—a city boy—stand it? He shivered uncontrollably.

After a while he stuck his head out from under the covers. The storm was lessening, but *they* were still out there. Very faintly, now that his grandfather had no need to shout any more, Tom could hear the muffled sound of his voice.

There was an interval of silence. He heard a scream from somewhere near the orchard. Another scream followed, fainter than the last.

The tension in Tom's chest loosened. They must be leaving, he thought. He had been spared.

The front door opened, and his grandfather entered. With him came the fresh smell of a departed storm. The other scent—the Swalalahist scent—was so faint as to be almost nonexistent.

"They're gone," Mr. Buche said simply.

Tom held the covers up to his chin. "Gone where, Grandfather? Where?

"Not now." The old man got into bed and turned on his side. "Now I'm going to sleep."

Tom, lying beside the sleeping form, considered getting up and going to his own bed. But he felt too exhausted by the evening's terror to make the effort.

The wind had died down. An occasional rumble far back in the mountains was the only sign that a storm had passed. It was strangely peaceful.

Tom felt his eyes grow heavy. His thoughts drifted. There was something familiar about the way his grandfather had spoken to the Swalalahist, he mused. It came to him that the old man spoke to him the same way.

Tom sighed, closed his eyes, and slept.

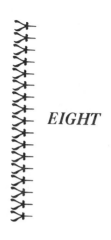

EIGHT

The letter from his mother came two days later. Although she was touched by his offer, she wrote, she just couldn't accept it.

As the days passed, the disappointment of his mother's refusal gradually diminished. Outside the facts that he missed his mother and Julie, and that sometimes he awoke at night covered with perspiration from a nightmare of screaming Swalalahist, living in the Cascade wilderness wasn't all that bad.

If there were after-school activities, Tom stayed overnight at Charlie's house. So he did not miss out on anything the school or the small town of Grindstone had to offer. He was even able to go to several movies and skating parties at Silvertown, which was located twelve miles south of Grindstone and was considerably larger.

And there were always things to do in the twenty acres of fenced area around the cabin. Now that the sun did not go down quite as early, he often fished in the creek after school. One Sunday afternoon, without his grandfather's knowledge, he even ventured a brief, icy swim.

His mother's letters continued cheerful—she was recovering faster than expected. Mostly, though, she was pleased that Tom and his grandfather were getting along so well. Tom wrote of the mountains and the wildlife, of school and his friends. He was careful to reread his letters to be sure no hint of the secret of the mountain had gotten into them.

The Swalalahist still figured in his life. Although they hadn't entered the yard since the night of the bad storm, he was awakened by their screams every so often. And each time fear would claim him.

His grandfather would get up and spend an hour or more somewhere outside before returning to bed. The strange scent of the Swalalahist would linger on the old man's jacket for a day or two and then be gone. Or if his grandfather took a jeep ride into the mountains, the scent would tell if he'd been with his Indian brothers.

Tom did not ask any more questions. And his grandfather in turn did not volunteer any new information.

Yet always a part of Tom's mind was aware of the Swalalahist. What or who were they? Devils? Monsters? Spirits of departed Indians? Or were they real? Could they be a band of outlaws from his grandfather's tribe? Maybe trying to scare people away from their hideout with screams and hideous disguises?

Only one person knew the answer. And even if that person were willing to tell him the truth, Tom didn't know if he wanted to hear.

He roamed the fenced-in area freely now. On this Saturday, the first day that hinted spring was not too far away, his grandfather asked at breakfast if Tom would check the fence for him. "Those deer have been eating my strawberry plants," he said. "There has to be a hole in the fence where they're getting in. But for the life of me I can't find it."

"Why don't you just let them stay in?" Tom asked. "Then when you need meat you wouldn't have to go out and hunt for it."

"I would never shoot a deer inside a fence." Mr. Buche started to gather the breakfast dishes from the table.

Tom jumped up to help. He should not have asked the question, he told himself. He should have realized that his grandfather respected the animals' freedom. "I'll find that fence hole," he promised. "Today."

"You do that. I have to saw up some wood. We're getting low."

Tom shut up a protesting Tilly with a bundle of hay. "Sorry, Tilly, but when I chase deer, I can't have you blatting and getting in my way."

Downwind from the deer, Tom crept up on them as they browsed beside the creek. The buck, still hornless, a doe, and her almost fully grown fawn were the same three Tom had been glimpsing inside the fence for the past two weeks.

Ears alert, unmoving, they stared at him.

"Get," Tom yelled. He clapped his hands together to frighten them.

They ran several feet and stopped. They stood, regarding him over their shoulders, waiting for his next move.

Tom scooped up a handful of pebbles and tossed it in their direction. "Move it."

They ran now in full flight, their graceful bodies bounding lightly through the underbrush.

Tom raced after them through the thickly for-

94

ested area. The buck found the eight-foot fence first and cleared it easily. The smaller doe followed, but her feet zinged against the top wire.

His grandfather had told him a deer would jump a deer fence if chased but would never jump to get inside an enclosure. So there had to be an opening. And the fawn, realizing it would have difficulty jumping the fence, now was frantically trying to find the place where it had entered.

To Tom it was great fun charging after the fawn. Even though stiff bottom branches tore at his hair and clothes, he didn't slow down. Always, ahead of him, he could hear the unseen deer breaking through the forest.

He heard the twang of the fence—then the sound of tiny hooves beating against the ground as the animal ran free on the other side.

The fawn had made good its escape. But he had been too far behind to tell if it had found the hole or in desperation had jumped the fence.

Well, it was up to him now to find the opening on his own. And he would, he vowed. Even if it took him all day. Painstakingly he searched the wire mesh, pressing himself between it and the tightly packed lower tree branches. Several times he came upon old deer trails leading to the fence.

But they led to old holes long since patched by his grandfather.

By midmorning he realized he was very thirsty. He had to return to the cabin for water.

"I was just going to look for you," his grandfather said. "I have to make a trip to Portland for a power saw part. Clean up."

A trip to the city—that was good news. It didn't take him long to get ready.

They ate hamburgers and milk shakes on the way, which was a big treat to Tom. In the city his grandfather surprised him by driving to a shopping center. In the largest department store he bought him two plaid shirts and two pairs of jeans. Tom wondered how his grandfather had known he favored this particular brand name. At his fervent expressions of thanks, the old man answered, "You needed them."

His grandfather made one other unexpected stop—a bookstore. He selected two books for himself and Tom chose one. The last store they went to handled the saw part which was what they had come after in the first place.

They didn't get home until four. After a hurry-up supper, his grandfather announced, "I've got to get at that saw."

"I'll look for the hole in the fence again."

The old man nodded absently as he undid the saw part from its wrappings.

Tom worked his way back to the place in the fence where he figured he'd left off checking. Then, being careful not to overlook any part of the wire mesh, he pushed aside brush and branches. Each fence length was scanned before he went on to the next. In his concentration he did not notice that the daylight was changing into twilight. Twigs and fir needles clung to his hair, his face was streaked with dirt, but still he continued to strain to see through the deepening shadows.

The deer had the best-hidden hole of all time, he mused as he struggled to pull back an especially unwieldy branch.

A faint rustle from the other side of the fence made him look up. Only the thick mesh of branches met his gaze. "Hey, deer!" He spoke toward where he'd heard the sound. "You're waiting for me to give up, huh? Forget it. My super-sharp eyes are going to find this fence hole. Tonight."

He realized then he didn't have much time left. The sun must be almost down. Only slivers of dull red light pierced the shadows.

Again he heard the rustling noise. "You want

97

to come in for your meal of strawberry leaves?" he asked, more now to hear himself talk than to impress the deer.

It was then he found the place. The fence had been pushed up from the bottom—a space just large enough for a deer to crawl through. *"Yippee,"* he exulted under his breath. *"Yippee."*

Grunting with the effort, he pulled the heavy wire mesh back into place.

The crunching sound from the other side of the fence began again. Nearer now. Definitely a deer. No small animal made that much noise walking through the forest.

He straightened. "Deer," he said cheerfully, "you're fresh out of luck." Pulling back a large fir branch, Tom strained to see through the woven wire where a faint ray of light still penetrated the gloom.

His grin froze.

Red glowing eyes in an ugly, mask-white face stared back at him.

Tom was too frightened to scream. Blindly, recklessly, he tore through the forest. Even when he'd made it to the clearing he didn't stop. He careened around the cabin to the lean-to where his grandfather sat working on the saw.

The old man stood up. He seemed to sense

98

what Tom had seen before he was told.

"A Swalalahist," Tom panted. "I saw a Swalalahist on the other side of the fence."

His grandfather's face showed a sadness that registered with Tom even in his fright.

The old man nodded his head and then sat down heavily on the stool he had just left. "I suppose it was bound to happen," he said wearily.

In his mind Tom saw again the horrible face, the red, glowing eyes. "Grandfather, I'm afraid."

"No one who has seen the Swalalahist has not been afraid."

Tom glanced toward the forest. "Will they come over the fence?"

"No. The only time they come in the yard is during a violent storm."

Tom glanced at the darkening sky. No clouds. No storms. At least tonight he was safe.

Later, lying in bed, he could not sleep. The red eyes of the Swalalahist seemed to burn in his mind. He tossed from side to side. He tried to think of Mom—of Julie—of fun at school. Still he saw the face.

The hours passed.

His grandfather's voice coming through the partition startled him. "Tom," he said. "Will you leave, too?"

The horrible face danced in Tom's mind. There was no room for any other thought. But his grandfather was waiting for an answer.

"I don't know," Tom whispered. "I don't know about anything."

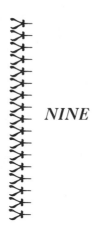

NINE

"For you, fellow." The postmaster handed Tom a letter across the counter.

As soon as he left the post office, Tom glanced at the store next door. Charlie hadn't come out yet, so Tom leaned against the building's wooden siding while he tore open the envelope.

"Just a note in haste," his mother wrote, "to tell you the good news. Doctor Porter really surprised me today. He said I could leave the hospital in June—with a bit of help, of course. He said I could do the exercises at home. Isn't that wonderful?"

Tom breathed in the cool mountain air. His mother was going to be O.K. He let his relief flood through him. And he could go home in June. The letter had come just at the right time.

102

He read on and his smile faded. "What would your grandfather say if Julie and I should come to Spirit Mountain for the summer? The insurance money would cover our expenses. I'd love to see the mountains—the tall firs—the deer—the creek—all the things you describe so well in your letters. But most of all I want to get to know your grandfather."

Tom shook his head vehemently. No way did he want his mother and Julie coming up here. No way did he want them to find out about the Swalalahist.

The letter continued, "I won't write to your grandfather about it until I hear what you think of the idea. It might be that you miss Los Angeles and would rather get back here pronto. If so, I would understand. Just so our family is together again. Always love, Mom."

"Just so our family is together again." Tom murmured the words. At the same time a small voice inside him whispered, "Grandfather is a part of my family now, too."

"Hey, you got a letter," Charlie said. "I hope it cheers you up. You haven't exactly been old smiley the last couple of days."

Tom grinned. "How's this?" he said. "Where's my popsicle?"

"Here you are. Fudge. And here's your change—six cents."

While they walked back to the school grounds, Tom considered telling Charlie he would be leaving in June. But that wouldn't be good news to Charlie, he reminded himself. He thought then of how he would miss Charlie—and Treena.

His grandfather. His chest constricted. It wouldn't be easy to tell him. Only three days ago after he'd seen the Swalalahist he'd had frantic thoughts about leaving Spirit Mountain. But now that he knew he actually could leave—in June—he wasn't sure. If only there weren't such a thing as the Swalalahist. . . . He started running. "Hey, Charlie," he called over his shoulder. "What's holding you up?"

They raced then in earnest. Tom arrived at the school first. He flopped full length on the lawn, holding the dripping popsicle aloft. A moment later Charlie threw himself down beside him. "I'd call it a tie, pardner," he panted.

"Call it anything you like, pardner," Tom drawled. "But I won."

At supper Tom kept sneaking glances at his grandfather. How should he tell him?

Mr. Buche leaned toward him, a twinkle glimmering in the dark eyes. "I found a set of old horseshoes today—tucked away in the lean-to. I put up stakes." He looked at Tom expectantly. "How about a game before we tackle the dishes?"

"Sure," Tom said. "It sounds like fun." He'd have plenty of time to tell him later. Maybe just before they went to bed.

Horseshoe playing *was* fun, Tom discovered. His grandfather, who said he hadn't played in many years, hadn't lost the knack. At first Tom's horseshoes went every which way, one almost beaning a disgusted Tilly. But after his grandfather showed him how to throw, Tom surprised himself by making several leaners. Then, even to his grandfather's surprise, he threw two ringers in a row.

Later, in the cabin, Tom decided it would be dumb to break the happy mood by saying anything about leaving. Time enough in the morning. There was no rush.

When he lay in bed, the Swalalahist face didn't come into his mind the way it had been doing.

Instead, Tom tried to imagine how it would be without his grandfather. He couldn't. The old man was always there—when he wanted to talk, when he had a question, when he needed help. And no matter what anyone said, he was the kindest, nicest person Tom had ever met. Tom was proud—very proud—of his Indian grandfather. He said it then, very low so it couldn't be heard beyond his room. "I wish I weren't leaving."

He was drifting into sleep when the scream came. Immediately he was wide awake. And immediately the same awful fear he'd felt when he'd first seen the red, glowing eyes flooded through him.

Mr. Buche was pulling on his mackinaw by the glow of the flashlight.

"Please don't go," Tom whispered.

Without looking at his grandson, the old man replied, "I must." He limped to the door and let himself out.

Tom made his way back to his room and got into bed. His grandfather thought more of the Swalalahist than of his own grandson, he fumed. He should have stayed when Tom asked him to. After all, it was only three days since the fright of seeing that face across the fence. His grandmother had left immediately when she'd seen one. And the old trapper had gone crazy . . .

When his grandfather returned, Tom was sitting up in bed waiting for him. "As soon as school is out I'm leaving," he announced. He pulled the covers up to his chin. Jaws clenched, he waited for the words that would try to dissuade him.

"Whatever you think is best." The old man turned toward his own room.

The next morning, a Friday, Tom told his grandfather in an offhand way that he needn't pick him up at the turnaround that evening. He was staying that night, and the weekend, too, at Charlie's house. Charlie's family had extended an open invitation to come whenever he wished.

After a restless night atop the double-decker bunk bed in Charlie's room, Tom decided he had not been fair to his grandfather. The old man was saddled with the trust of the Indian devils, so what could he do? Hold his crybaby grandson's hand all night? And there was also the grimmer possibility that, if his grandfather didn't go outside, the Swalalahist might attack the cabin. That the old man was protecting him.

Tom resolved that as soon as he saw his grandfather he would explain the real reason he was leaving. And that it had nothing to do with his grandfather's going outside to the Swalalahist when Tom had begged him not to. And it would be important also to explain he wasn't leaving because he'd seen that awful face either.

Riding home in the bus on Monday evening,

all Tom could think of was that he'd been gone for four days. Something could have happened to his grandfather in the meantime. But the red jeep was waiting. He scrambled in hastily. "Hi," he said.

"Hello, Tom."

Their eyes met. In that brief contact, Tom saw how much his grandfather had missed him.

The jeep jerked into motion. And now Tom told about the letter. That his mother would leave the hospital in June, which was almost unbelievable. In the beginning there had been doubt she would ever walk again. So to be with his mother was the real reason he was going home.

"Thank God for your mother's healing," the old man murmured. "If only she and your little sister could live here on Spirit Mountain—with us." He shook his head. "A beautiful dream— no more than that."

Tom felt himself flush. It was as if his grandfather had read his mind—or his mother's letter. He reached into his jacket pocket. The letter was still there.

He settled back into the bucket seat. He should feel happy, he thought. His mother was almost well, he was going home in June, and his grandfather understood. Instead, all he felt was a strange feeling of sadness—of emptiness.

On the following weekends Mr. Buche took Tom on trips to places of interest. He told his grandson, "We'd better get in all of the Northwest sights we can before you return to Los Angeles."

One day they went to the Oregon Museum of Science and Industry. Another day they toured the Portland Art Museum.

Tom noted that his grandfather, away from Spirit Mountain and the small town of Grindstone, was invariably treated with deference. His bearing, his native dignity, and his Indian dress made him an imposing figure. In Grindstone the old man exchanged a minimum of words with the store keeper and the garage owner. And Tom had only seen him nod at the postmaster, never speak. Away from the town, Mr. Buche spoke readily and with authority.

One day his grandfather, in a somber mood, took him to a museum with historical exhibits from the early days of Oregon.

After they had looked at most of the exhibits, including some exotic Indian masks, his grandfather led him to one of the glass-enclosed cases.

Yellowed newspapers were on display. "I brought you here to see this," the old man said. "Then later you will understand."

Tom had to put his face near the glass to read the small, faded print:

After much unrest between the Indian tribe of Spirit Mountain and the settlers of the area, General Cooper (Retired, Army) and his volunteer settler army invited the Indian men to come to a peace meeting at Portage.

The Indians, believing there would be an end to the killing, went willingly enough. After all instruments of weaponry were checked at the door, the Indians were ushered into the large log meetinghouse located at Portage. As soon as the redskins were seated, the general ordered the doors locked from the outside.

Then the white men opened fire on the Indians through the windows. None of the redskins made their escape.

The corpses of the slain men were thrown into an excavation which had been dug previous to the arrival of the Indians. The next day the old men, women, and children who were left on Spirit Mountain were started on a month's march to a reservation provided by the government in the southern Oregon territory. General Cooper was of the opinion that the settler army had acquitted themselves very well.

The only Indian not included in the march to the reservation was the squaw, Molly Buche. Her French trapper husband, Pierre Buche, was away at the time of the shooting incident, and he only returned in time to save his wife and child from being taken with the others.

Tom reread the chilling paragraphs. He looked up at his grandfather. "Were any of your relatives killed in the massacre?"

The old man's face was grim. "Yes, my relatives—and yours."

Tom moved to the next case. His eyes mechanically read the caption: "Brave Indian Fighter," below the picture of a blond, bearded man. He turned abruptly to his grandfather. "Let's get out of here," he said.

Another Saturday they drove to Mount Hood. And, although there were only scanty patches of snow around Timberline Lodge because of the record dry winter, Tom enjoyed the day. They went to the coast and he looked in vain for the Japanese glass balls which sometimes drifted across the ocean to wash up on the beaches.

They went to the zoo. "For your benefit," his grandfather said. He, himself, hated seeing the animals caged. "Cruelty," he called it. And, because of his Indian grandfather, Tom saw it as cruelty too. He decided he never wanted to return.

On their trips Tom found he was always learning something new. While driving he enjoyed it most when he could coax the old man to talk of his childhood and his spunky Indian mother and how she had clung to the Indian ways. Sometimes his grandfather would start to say something, and then he would stop abruptly. Tom guessed he had been about to mention the Swalalahist.

Tom never questioned him. The Indian devils had caused enough trouble between them. He did not want that again. In fact, he wanted nothing at all to do with the Swalalahist. Still, when he was on Spirit Mountain, thoughts of them kept popping into his mind.

Unless he was with his grandfather he didn't venture near the fence. Even though he had not lost his mind like the trapper, he never wanted to see another Swalalahist—ever again. The face of the one he had seen would be photographed on his mind forever, he figured.

The days drifted toward spring. Tom found himself saying silent good-byes—to the creek, to the mountains, to the tree in the yard which made such a good lookout. Every day he noticed something else he would miss. He found he could not tell the kids at school, not even Charlie and Treena, that he would be leaving in June. And Tom and his grandfather did not speak about it any more, either.

If only there weren't any Swalalahist, Tom thought, I could stay here in the mountains. And Mom and Julie could live here, too. If only. . .

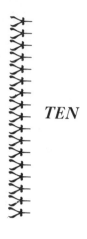

TEN

The longest winter dry spell in the recorded history of the Northwest came to an abrupt end.

"A change in the weather," Grandfather predicted at supper one night. Expectantly he turned on the radio.

"Good news, folks," the weatherman said. "You thought it wouldn't happen, didn't you? Well, tonight, be prepared. It's going to get cold—and colder. And get this, folks, snow in the mountains tomorrow for that needed snowpack. That's where we get our summer water supply, remember?"

The temperature dropped suddenly during the night. Tom had to get up and put on two extra quilts.

In the morning it was five below zero.

"I can smell the snow," Mr. Buche said. "It won't be long now. No school for you today. I can't take any chances on your getting snowed out."

"O.K. by me. I can work on my birdhouse." Tom felt a rush of anticipation at the thought of a whole day to complete his assigned craft project.

After breakfast his grandfather took the rifle from its rack. "We're getting low on meat. I'd better take a quick trip up the mountain after a deer. We'll have fresh liver tonight. Sound good to you?"

Tom grunted in reply. Although his grandfather considered deer liver a delicacy, he had never acquired the taste.

"I'll be back by noon," his grandfather promised. "Keep up the fire. It's going to get still colder. And the snow is going to fly." His pleasure in the weather change was apparent in his voice.

Tom braved the icy air to wave until the jeep disappeared from sight behind the orchard.

The crackling of the fire in the wood stove a cozy backdrop of sound, Tom spent the morning contentedly working on the birdhouse. He measured carefully. In his mind he heard his grandfather say, "Take your time—do good work." He

115

sawed. And then nailed. When the pieces of wood were fitted together, there were no gaps. "Birds," he said with satisfaction, "you're going to have one elegant house."

Now that he had finished the most exacting stage of the building, he got up and stretched. He became aware of hunger. He had been so involved he had not even snacked.

Tom looked at the clock. Where was his grandfather? He'd said he'd be back by noon. Yet here it was twelve-thirty. His grandfather always followed through on his promises. If he said he'd do something, he did it. Tom remembered then. The old man had also said he'd bring back a deer liver. The cold must have driven the deer back into the mountains. Grandfather wasn't going to have a quick trip after all.

Tom went to the window and looked out. His breath quickened. Snowflakes were drifting silently down. A sprinkling of white covered the frozen ground. How he wished his grandfather were with him to share in the excitement of the snow.

After a quick lunch, he shingled the birdhouse. Finished with that, he improvised on the original design. He made a small porch, also shingled, and then a chimney.

116

The final step and the most fun was the painting. For the house he chose a rich shade of brown; for the shingles and details, a contrasting orange.

When he had finished he stepped back to admire the effect. It was the best-looking birdhouse he'd ever seen. Flushed with his success, he imagined his grandfather's reaction. He looked at the clock.

How could the time have gone so fast? It was almost six. Grandfather had never returned this late before, even when he'd gone in the afternoon.

Now it was snowing in earnest. The view from the window was partly hidden by a mass of swirling flakes. The ground and trees, dimly seen, were covered with the stuff. "Where are you, Grandfather?" he said aloud.

When he turned from the window Tom realized he was shivering. The cabin had become chilly. He opened the stove door. Only a few coals glowed on the bottom of the grate. "Dummy," he chided himself. "You almost let it go out."

After he put in pitch-streaked kindling, the fire flared bravely. He put on heavier pieces. The flame diminished and then died. He blew with all his might. Smoke rolled from the open stove door and stung his eyes. But resolutely he continued to blow until a sudden flare-up of flame rewarded his efforts. He rested and then blew again. The fire burned brightly. Relieved, Tom closed the stove door. Now the fire hummed steadily, muted.

It was then he became aware of the plaintive bleating of Tilly. She needed to be milked. Since Grandfather wasn't here he'd have to do it himself. He put on his warm outerwear, at the last moment replacing his own knit stocking cap with his grandfather's fur hat with earflaps.

Tilly was beside herself with joy when he entered the icy-cold shed. But he had no time for play. "I hope I remember how this goes," he told her. He sat down on the milking stool and rested his head against the goat's warm flank.

His first efforts met with success. The familiar *ping, ping* of the milk hitting the bottom of the bucket reminded him of the many different things he had learned from his grandfather. But there wouldn't be much demand for his goat-milking skills in Los Angeles, he thought.

Tilly taken care of, Tom returned to the cabin. He stomped the snow from his boots before he entered. The warmth of the kitchen felt good. For a few moments he held his hands over the stove while he considered what he could get ready for supper. His grandfather would be cold when he returned, that was for sure. First a pot of coffee, he decided.

He made it plenty strong, the way his grandfather liked it. When it boiled it smelled somehow comforting—as if his grandfather were nearby, ready to pour a cup for himself.

He peeled potatoes—more than usual. Grandfather would be very hungry. He covered them with cold water. If he fried them before the liver, they would get soggy.

The clock ticked away. Seven-fifteen now. He poured himself a cup of coffee. The first sip burnt his tongue, and he set the cup down to cool. If he turned on the radio he'd get the weather.

The national news was still on—all bad. The Portland news was no better. A bank robbery. A factory fire. Several house fires caused by overheated stove pipes. And then the weather. The late-season cold snap was causing hardships. Snow to continue through the night.

He tried to look out the window. But because of the snowflakes plastered against the glass, he could not see anything.

The coffee was now too cold, he found, when

119

he sat down again at the table. And bitter. With a grimace he returned the cup to the table.

He should eat something, he told himself. Rummaging through the cupboard, he spotted a box of raisins. He poured himself a handful and then walked over to his grandfather's favored rocking chair. He stood looking at it for several moments before he let himself down into its cane-bottomed seat.

He ate the raisins one by one. When he had finished, he got up to examine his birdhouse. It was just a birdhouse, he thought. Probably half the kids in the class had made one as good—or better.

The cold seemed to be seeping through the cracks around the doors and windows. He put more wood into the stove. Then he turned the radio to a country western station. Just as quickly, he turned it off. He didn't want to miss hearing the jeep's motor when it came into the yard.

The radio's silence suddenly made the room with its long jagged shadows appear sinister. Hastily Tom turned the radio on again. It came to him then that this was the first time he had been alone in the cabin after dark.

He reminded himself that there was a new copy

of *Popular Science* he had intended to read after supper. Since supper was going to be very late, he had better read it right now. He turned pages without really seeing. When he had finished leafing through the magazine, he started over again. All the time his ears strained above the radio music—strained to hear the jeep's motor.

At nine-thirty he made himself a peanut butter sandwich. But he found he could not eat more than half. At ten he turned out the lamp and went to bed. Grandfather would be sorry, he told himself. He'd feel guilty that he'd left him alone so long.

But would he ever return? Tom twisted his head from side to side on the pillow. What was the use of pretending? Something had happened to his grandfather. He had known it since he'd looked at the clock when it was almost six.

Now very clearly in his mind he saw the old man lying in the dense snow-covered forest, his face and body stained with blood. The deer had not been killed after all—only wounded. And when his grandfather had gone to claim it, the deer had risen and attacked him with its sharp hooves. He had heard of this occurring. Not likely, he told himself. Grandfather was too expe-

121

rienced a hunter to let that happen to him.

Perhaps a cougar had dropped out of a tree when Grandfather was riding underneath in the jeep. Not likely either. The jeep would have frightened the cougar away.

How about if he had fallen and broken his leg in the woods? That could be possible. But then Grandfather would have splinted the leg himself and driven home. He would not have let a broken leg stop him.

His breath caught. There was only one answer.

The terrible Swalalahist whom his grandfather had trusted had turned on him!

Hurriedly Tom got up and dressed. Not rocking, he sat in the old rocker and considered what to do. He had to get help. But how?

It would be too dangerous to leave the fenced-in enclosure at night. On the other side of the gate were the Swalalahist. And, even if he could get by them, how could he walk the miles of snow-clogged trail to Charlie's house in a freezing blizzard in the dark without getting lost?

He shook his head in despair. There was nothing to do—nothing to do but wait until it got light.

Then Charlie's father would notify the sheriff's

office. They would send out a search party to look for his grandfather. They had to. It was their duty—even if the person they were searching for was feared and hated and called the devil man. They just had to.

Tom thought of the Swalalahist's face—and his assurance dissolved. What defense had any human against such creatures?

Shivering, he turned on the radio. Several times he thought he heard the jeep's motor and turned it off. But it was only the wind in the chimney, or an animal howling far off.

After the eleven o'clock news, he determined to get some sleep. It would be a long hike in the morning and he had to be rested.

But it was no use. As he lay in bed, eyes shut, he could envision his grandfather's torn and bleeding body. The Swalalahist were gathered around their victim, chanting gibberish.

He clambered out of bed. He had lost too much time already. His grandfather had to be helped now—before it was too late. If he bundled up good he could keep from freezing.

Over his pajama top he pulled on two sweaters. Over his pajama bottoms, two pairs of pants. Next his jacket. His boots. Then the fur hat. In his

123

grandfather's closet he found a pair of gloves, much too large but reassuringly warm. The flashlight clutched firmly in one hand, he opened the door. Blowing snow met him head on.

He had gotten only a few steps from the cabin before he realized the snow was now even with his boot tops. He plunged ahead, the light's beam reflecting a solid shield of white.

Tilly must have heard him. Her forlorn bleating issued from the shed, becoming fainter as he struggled on. He lunged in and out of drifts. With a single-minded concentration he managed to stay in the faint twin indentations he knew to be the ruts made by the jeep.

One time he did wander off the trail. It took him several minutes of searching with the flashlight before he found it again. He walked on, becoming more and more aware of the stinging cold. It even made his chest hurt.

How come he had never realized before that the cabin was such a long distance from the gate? he wondered. The idea grew then that he must have wandered off the trail again. That he was walking in circles.

When he recognized the ghostly outlines of the orchard he became calmer. He was all right, he told himself. He had only to follow the trail—to the gate—and then on to Charlie's house. He would make it.

Other snow-covered humps were not immediately recognizable. He was sure he was off the trail again when the light beam hit what looked like a wall of white. Too late his momentum carried him into the drift. A shower of snow cascaded over him, accompanied by the zinging of the fence wire. Finally. He'd found the gate.

The gate resisted his efforts to move it. With his hands he scooped away snow. But it seemed to him the snow was coming down so fast he was barely keeping even. He straightened up and tackled the gate again. By tugging and lifting he forced it open just far enough for him to squeeze through.

Realization came to him—making his knees suddenly weak. *He* was outside the gate. Where were *they*?

Were they lurking behind the giant snow-laden trees? Were hundreds of red glowing eyes trained on him, watching his every struggling step?

He forced himself to stay where he was while he fought his panic.

After a few moments he straightened his shoul-

ders. He had to go on. There was no going back. He was the only person who could get help for his grandfather.

The feeling that he was being watched as strong as ever, Tom plunged ahead into the snow-filled darkness.

ELEVEN

The thought came to him that he was doing O.K. It was then he stumbled over a hidden log. He fell, the flashlight flying through the air and landing some distance from the trail. In his haste to get the light, he became entangled in underbrush.

Freeing himself, he retrieved the light. But he found he had lost his bearings. Everything identifiable had vanished in the snow.

He forgot all caution in his urgency to find the trail again. He ran head on into a low-hanging branch.

Stunned by the pain he lunged away from the tree. But everywhere he turned were other trees. Panic rose through the creeping numbness of cold and fatigue. "I have to get to Charlie's," he told himself. "I just *have* to."

As he struggled on, a tree snag's dead, uplifted root caught his foot. In trying to right himself, he twisted his ankle and went down.

Tom sat there until the worst of the pain subsided. An attempt to rise failed and he sank back into the snow again. He was very tired, he realized, more tired than he'd ever been before in his life. He wished he could stay right where he was and never get up. He remembered then about people who had frozen to death doing exactly that.

His arms flailing the air, he got himself upright. A sharp stab of pain shot through his ankle, and he almost lost his footing again. But he stayed on his feet.

Everywhere he aimed the flashlight's beam it was the same. Trees and more trees.

Try to figure things out, he told himself. The snow should be blowing from the north, and you want to go southwest. When you first went off the trail after the flashlight, you went south. Now if you go northwest, you should find the trail again.

He turned to face where he thought northwest should be. Careful of the sharp, dead bottom branches, he worked his way around tree trunks.

130

Unexpectedly he found himself in a clearing. He plunged in and out of drifts, sure he would find the trail momentarily. But all the continuously moving light beam showed was the silent, falling snow.

Tom stopped. Tears of frustration rolled slowly from his eyes and within minutes froze on his cheeks. "It's no use," he said aloud. The fatigue he had been fighting seemed to overwhelm him. He began walking again, but each step took all his will power. Yet he forced himself on.

When his feet slipped out from under him he was too tired to catch himself. He fell then, rolling over and over down a steep incline. At length his body came to rest against an outcropping of snow-padded rock.

He felt incapable of making an attempt to rise. Still there was no pain. Not in his ankle. Not in his body. Not anywhere. It was as if he were made of wood. I am going to freeze to death, he thought. But he didn't move.

He heard it then, the *crunch, crunch* of someone or something coming down the hill where he had just fallen. "Get up," he mumbled. "You've got to get up."

He struggled groggily to his feet. He was able

to take two steps before he went down again. "Grandfather has to have help," he murmured. But this time he did not get up.

His arm leadenly lifted the flashlight.

He saw what he'd expected to see—red glowing eyes.

His arm dropped back to the snow. And he switched off the light.

The faint dread smell of the Swalalahist drifted to his nostrils. Wearily he closed his eyes, hoping the Swalalahist would go away.

But the footsteps, heavy and deliberate, came ever nearer. The smell, strong now, enveloped him in its strangeness.

He felt his stomach contract. He was able to turn his face to one side before he was sick.

Then he lay there, too exhausted to move, too exhausted to care.

He felt himself being picked up as lightly as if he were an infant. Weakly he struggled to get free. But his arms were pinned against his sides. He did remember to keep a grip on the flashlight.

Then the trip began. Tom felt himself borne fleetly, the frozen snow crackling under the giant impact of the Swalalahist. The creature seemed to run up hills too steep for a human to climb, then descend into rugged gorges and as swiftly make its way out of them, and on up into the mountains.

Is this another nightmare? Tom wondered. Is this one time when I can't wake up?

It seemed like hours until they reached a destination. The narrow blackness of a cave stood out against a snow-covered cliff. Before they entered, Tom caught the strong Swalalahist odor coming out to meet him. Then he was among them. The warmth of many bodies, the chattering of many voices surrounded him in the pitch darkness.

He felt himself lowered onto some kind of soft material. The Swalalahist let go of him then.

He lay where he had been placed, still clutching the unlit flashlight, too weak from fright and exposure to move. But then his finger, seemingly of its own volition, switched on the light.

Instantly the cavern sprang to life with, it seemed to Tom, hundreds of red, glowing eyes.

A scream echoed and reechoed against the rock walls. Before it faded away, Tom realized it was his own voice.

They gathered around him chattering excitedly.

Now in the flashlight's beam he recognized them for what they were. How come he hadn't guessed what they were before? he wondered.

He answered his own question: Because he had never really believed there were such monsters.

Giants—standing upright—some of them ten feet tall, the larger ones weighing at least a ton. Coarse brown hair covered their heavy bodies. But their fearsome faces, rough skinned and white, were hairless.

There were male and female, some of the females with infants clasped to their breasts. The young, of different sizes, were the most curious. They felt of Tom's face and clothing while he lay sprawled on a pile of moss and sticks that had been hollowed into a crude nest. One and then another of the young tumbled into the nest with him. Soon the moss bed was full of wriggling small-sized Swalalahist, all touching him.

Tom shrank away from their hands. When they tried to take the flashlight from him, he hit at them with it. There was much back and forth chattering. Then, to Tom's relief, they all vacated the nest.

The largest of the males—the one Tom sensed had brought him here—now approached to touch his face. The male's interest quickly switched to the flashlight. With strong fingers he pried it loose from Tom's hand. He walked away, causing the light's beam to tilt haphazardly across the cave's interior. The light illuminated the domed ceiling and then swept low to reveal many more rough nests strewn across the hard-packed dirt floor.

Then the light rested for a moment on something not as innocent—a pile of large and small bones. Tom drew a ragged breath. Eaters of men. It must be true.

Now tensely alert, his gaze followed the light. Where was the entrance? Several openings were visible. They could be doorways to other caverns and lead nowhere. But one of them had to be a passageway to the outside.

The light swooped toward the ceiling, then down and across the floor into the farthermost corner from where Tom lay.

He jerked his head to follow the beam. He was sure he had seen something red among the dull browns and blacks of the cave. Something red— in that far corner.

He watched intently, following the light's every move. The large male was now sitting on the floor. Seeming to lose interest in the flashlight, he flung it some distance from him.

Immediately a young Swalalahist ran to it and grabbed it. The beam zigzagged across the cavern. Several other young ones tried to take the flashlight from the first one, and a spirited game of takeaway started.

Tom kept his gaze on the nest in the corner where he'd seen the red color. The light touched the nest several times. Tom drew a deep breath. He was sure. Very sure. The red was his grandfather's mackinaw.

The young ones became weary of their game. The flashlight was discarded. It now lay on the floor next to the big male. He ignored it for several minutes. Then he picked it up and, his body casting a huge shadow, he walked to the far corner. He placed the light on the edge of the nest. Chattering softly, he lifted a limp, mackinaw-clad body and then let it drop back on the moss.

Tom sat up. He had had a brief glimpse of his grandfather's face. It was streaked with dried blood. Grief welled up in him. The Swalalahist have killed him, he thought.

His own safety didn't matter any more. Tom stood up. For a moment he teetered back and forth. The attack of dizziness conquered, he lurched across the cave to his grandfather.

The huge male that had been crouching by the nest straightened and stood up. Tom did not waver. If he were going to be killed he would die beside his grandfather. He picked up the flashlight and by its light looked down into the silent face. He was aware the Swalalahist were gathering around him again, but he did not glance their way.

TWELVE

The blood came from a large wound on his grand-father's temple. When Tom moved the old man's head to see better, the wound bled anew. Feeling a sudden stirring of hope, Tom bent to put his ear to the mackinaw-covered chest. Although the Swalalahist, because of their milling around, were making too much noise for him to hear a heart-beat, he felt the faint up and down movement of the chest.

He faced the Swalalahist. "Stay away," he said, his voice unsteady. "He's alive."

One of the Swalalahist, a female with gray-streaked hair, reached out and touched his face. He jerked his head away. "Get back," he shouted, swinging the flashlight in a menacing manner.

They moved back a few feet. When he swung

the flashlight again, they retreated some distance away. There they chattered among themselves.

Tom climbed into the bed of moss and sticks. He sat, back straight, the flashlight trained in the direction of the Swalalahist. He would protect his grandfather to the death, he resolved.

The Swalalahist, still casting glances at Tom, retired to the far corner of the cave where they huddled together. But as time went on they seemed to lose interest in the boy. One after another they left the cave or curled up in sleep. Finally Tom was the only one awake.

Even in these nightmare circumstances he kept feeling himself falling asleep too. His head would nod forward, and he would jerk awake. Eventually, giving in to the inevitable, he lay down next to his grandfather, his arm flung protectively across the old man's chest.

Tom awakened to the racket of Swalalahist screams and whistles. Pale gray light partly illuminated the cave. He scrambled to sit up, prepared for the worst.

"So, you are awake at last," a voice next to him said.

Tom looked into his grandfather's face incredulously. "You feel O.K.?"

His grandfather smiled ruefully. "I've felt better."

"Did the Swalalahist attack you?"

"Attack me?" He shook his head and then winced in pain. "Never would the Swalalahist hurt me. The jeep slid off the trail in the snow and hit a boulder. I must have lost consciousness."

"How'd you get here?"

"Tooka, I suppose." He pointed to the large male, the one Tom thought had brought him. "He was running alongside the jeep at the time."

Tooka, when he heard his name spoken, came to the old man and touched his face.

Mr. Buche, as if it were a ritual, touched Tooka's face in return. "Tooka and I were practically raised together," he told his grandson. "We played right here while my mother gathered roots and berries. Shul, the old female over there, watched over us a lot of the time."

Shul, she of the gray-streaked hair, craned her head forward on hearing her name. She came to them. Gently she touched his grandfather's face. He returned the greeting.

Now Tom understood. He started to laugh. It was all too crazy. He laughed and laughed and couldn't seem to stop.

His grandfather, face concerned, put his arm around his grandson's shoulders. It was then Tom began to cry.

The Swalalahist gathered around. An embarrassed Tom hiccuped to a stop.

Tooka bent then and touched Tom's cheek. It seemed natural for Tom to reach up and touch Tooka's fearsome face.

Now the others—and in the half-light Tom saw there were more like forty than a hundred—went through the touching ritual with him. Then several curiously felt of his hair.

"They've never seen blond hair before," Mr. Buche said with a smile. "Enough," he said and clapped his hands. They scampered away as if it were a command they'd heard many times.

"Why did Tooka bring me here?" Tom asked.

His grandfather shrugged. "Who knows? Sometimes I think they're almost human. They seem to sense the right thing to do."

Tom's face mirrored his shock. *"Aren't* they human? They walk upright like people."

"If only they were. Then they could protect themselves from man."

Tom looked straight at his grandfather. "They're Bigfeet, aren't they?"

The old man nodded. "Yes, known as Bigfoot

142

in the Cascades, known as Sasquatch in Canada. Known by different names in different areas. This particular family living on Spirit Mountain acquired the name of Swalalahist or Indian devils."

"Why such an awful name?"

The old man rubbed his chin. "It's an unlikely story," he said, "but it happens to be true. When the first mountain man wandered up here, he spotted several of the Swalalahist. Later, when he recounted what he had seen, he described them as, 'Big, hairy Indian creatures who ran like the devil was chasing them.' Those very words are on record in the library. And so the name—Indian devils."

"I still don't like it."

"The Indians didn't care for it either. But, because it had enough scare value to keep non-Indians off the mountain, our ancestors in subtle ways promoted it."

Just then one of the smallest of the Swalalahist cautiously approached them. Tom's grandfather put an arm around the little creature and continued, "Most often when there have been sightings of Bigfoot—in Oregon, California, Canada—there have also been reports of shooting at them."

"Why did they want to kill them?"

"Out of fear. Remember how the Indians of Spirit Mountain were massacred? Because of mindless fear." The old man paused reflectively. "In the last ten years there is a new threat—hunters and scientists who want to be the first with proof. Proof being Bigfoot bodies. There are even rewards for parts of bodies."

"Didn't they get proof? Didn't someone take a film of them?"

"Yes, men in California. But the scientists want more."

"What about all the reports from people who've seen Bigfoot?"

"Ha, reports don't mean much to scientists. They say people with wild imaginations make them up. Look at the gorilla. Do you know the scientific world wouldn't admit there was a gorilla until 1847? And yet there had been reports about the species for over four hundred years."

Tom took the hand of the small Swalalahist and drew the little body toward him. He noted that in the daylight the eyes were amber.

The little one grasped Tom's finger, and then it timidly crawled into his lap.

Tom automatically put his arms around the furry body snuggling against his chest. The funny little white face looked up at him, its eyes filled

144

with trust. Tom felt an unexpected warmth flow through him, and his arms tightened.

"The Swalalahist are affectionate and peaceful," his grandfather said. "But if it were discovered they were here, wintering in this cave, you may be sure Bigfoot hunters would be here immediately, shooting and capturing them. What they wouldn't kill, they'd put in cages."

Realization dawned on Tom. "Grandfather, when you run off hunters and timber buyers with a gun, you are really *protecting* the Swalalahist!"

The old man nodded his head. "You understand now. I must be on guard constantly. Since I am the last of my tribe, I have to keep the trust by myself—to keep the knowledge of the Swalalahist of Spirit Mountain from those who would kill and exploit them."

"But you are not the last," Tom said.

His eyes serious, the old man regarded Tom. "You had better think it over well before you make any decision about the trust." He paused. "It's not an easy life."

It wouldn't be easy, Tom reflected. He would never be able to confide in *anyone* about the Swalalahist—not even friends like Charlie and Treena. And when people called his grandfather—and perhaps himself in later years—"devil man," he would have no defense. He would have to remain silent.

The small Swalalahist touched his face. Tom looked down at it and with sudden resolve at his grandfather.

He caught his breath. In the strengthening morning light he could see more clearly the old man's injuries.

All thought of the Swalalahist trust left his mind. "You've got to get to a doctor, Grandfather," he said. "You sure have an awful-looking bump on your head."

Mr. Buche's hand found the swelling, and he grimaced. But his smile was meant to be reassuring. "I'm feeling better all the time," he said. As if to prove his point, he struggled to his feet. "Just a little stiff," he admitted. "No need for a doctor."

Tom was not to be put off that easily. He placed the young Swalalahist on its feet; then, he, himself, stood up. "We have to get that jeep upright and running."

"No problem. You may be sure this isn't the first time the jeep tangled with a boulder on this mountain."

Tom's voice was aghast. "This has happened to you before? Up here all alone?"

146

Mr. Buche's hand indicated the Swalalahist. "Not alone."

The Swalalahist, as if they sensed he was speaking about them, gathered around.

Tom was going to answer, "A lot of help they'd be." But then it came to him that neither he nor his grandfather would be alive if the huge animals hadn't come to their rescue the previous night.

"That's right," he said softly. "You weren't alone."

When they started to leave the cave, the Swalalahist went with them. Tom had a moment's fear he and his grandfather might be crushed by the press of the enormous bodies crowding around them. But the animals never touched them even at the cave's narrow exit.

Outside, the sun shone brightly and the air was crystal clear. Several Swalalahist were capering in drifts of snow. The white stuff had already been packed down at the cave's entrance and numerous footprints led into the white-blanketed forest.

Tom looked at the snow in consternation. "How will we ever get through this stuff to the jeep?" he asked.

Mr. Buche's eyes twinkled. "We already have the snowplows." He called, "Tooka. Koia."

Not only Tooka and the equally large Koia but all the other Swalalahist responded—even the females with small infants at their breasts. They led the way through the snow as if they knew Mr. Buche and Tom's destination.

"You're right about the snowplows," said Tom. "Now if they could only help us with the jeep."

"They will."

They found the jeep about half a mile from the cave. It was tilted against a boulder and almost covered by a deep snowdrift.

Under Mr. Buche's directions, and guided by ropes as if they were a team of horses, Tooka and Koia righted the jeep. Then in a swirl of dislodged snow the two animals pulled the vehicle onto the barely discernible road. While this task was being accomplished, the other Swalalahist screamed and whistled in seemingly high spirits, their voices carrying up and down the mountains in the clear, cold air.

Tom, standing back to watch, could only marvel. It's true, he thought. Grandfather never was alone.

Mr. Buche heaved the discarded ropes into the rear of the jeep and then climbed inside. "Come on, Tom," he called. "We're moving on out."

148

Tom, jolted from his thoughts, hastily scrambled into the bucket seat.

His grandfather stepped on the starter. When the jeep motor roared into action, Tom sighed his relief. "I was afraid it wouldn't start," he admitted.

"If it had been tipped more on its side it wouldn't have," the old man said. "The battery acid would have run out."

"I guess luck stays with you, Grandfather."

The old man gave his grandson a level glance. "Not luck," he said, his voice low, "but God— our great protector." Reaching out a brown, sinewy hand, he shifted the jeep into gear.

Skillfully, over the barest outline of road, he steered the car, the tire chains making hardly any noise in the soft powdered snow.

Tom was glad that several of the larger Swalalahist decided to accompany them. Tooka and Koia took it upon themselves to run in front of the jeep. The others, more playful, ran sometimes in front, sometimes at the side, and sometimes behind them.

Tom was especially grateful for the animals' presence when snowdrifts made the road impassable at several places and they had to dig their way out. The companionable chatter of the Swala-lahist as he and his grandfather shoveled snow was oddly comforting. It wasn't as if an old man and a boy were all alone in the vast, snow-clogged wilderness.

But within sight of the gate the animals, as if by a signal, stopped. Mr. Buche braked the jeep. He spoke a few Indian words to the Swalalahist. Then the jeep jerked into motion again.

Screaming and whistling, the animals headed back up the mountain.

Tom felt a vague sense of loss now that they had departed. He shrugged. He had a pressing problem to face—getting his grandfather to the doctor.

At the fence Mr. Buche idled the motor. "We're here. How's about opening the gate?"

Tom resolutely shook his head. "We're going to Silvertown to the doctor."

Mr. Buche made a face. "I haven't been to a doctor for nigh onto fifty years."

Tom made his voice firm. "You're going now."

His grandfather rubbed his chin. "You win," he said finally. "I guess the only way I can get out of opening that gate myself is to keep moving."

The snow was not nearly as deep at the lower

elevations, and the jeep was able to make good progress all the way to Silvertown.

After tests at the doctor's office, Mr. Buche was pronounced, "fit as a fiddle." The doctor regarded the old man admiringly. "You are a very healthy man for your age," he said. "A bump on the head won't hold you down for long."

On the ride home from Silvertown, Tom's mind fastened on the question of the trust of protecting the Swalalahist again. It would be very hard, he conceded. After his grandfather died, he would be the only one left.

Impatiently he jerked himself into a more upright position. What was he thinking about? He wasn't an orphan. There was Mom—she really cared about people, and animals too. And there was Julie. His mind leaped ahead. Perhaps, by the time he grew up, others might help too.

Already a lot of people were becoming concerned about the environment and clean air—and they were doing something about it. Maybe, before too long, everyone would come to realize what a wonderful world they lived in and not be so dumb about hurting each other—or caging up wild animals.

It just might happen that they would be as concerned as his grandfather and himself about pro-

151

tecting the Swalalahists' freedom to live on Spirit Mountain undisturbed.

But first something would have to be done to make this change in people's attitudes come about. What could he, Tom Buche, do to help? He bit his lower lip. Why couldn't everyone be like Grandfather? Or Mom? Or Julie, even?

He remembered then—Mom and Julie. He had a question to ask. "Grandfather," he said. "Would you mind if Mom and Julie came here in June? They'd like to stay for a while."

A smile slowly formed on the old man's lips. "I can't think of anything I'd like more," he finally said. "I hope your mother and my granddaughter stay a long time." He paused. "It would make me even happier if all of you made this your home."

Tom caught his breath. Everything was working out. Like a jigsaw puzzle. "I'd sure like that," he said aloud. Then a new thought came to him—lack of money. "But Mom couldn't work here," he confessed. "We wouldn't have enough to live on."

The old man threw back his head and laughed. "You never have to worry about that. Here's another secret. I have plenty of money. All it does is earn interest. Let's put some of it to use now.

And later"—he stopped to smile at Tom—"when the time comes, you may be sure there will be sufficient to send you and your sister to good universities. Education is very important." He paused, and then, as if weighing each word, he added, "To help make this world a better place."

Of course, thought Tom. His grandfather had given him the answer. An education—a really good education. So that he would have the credentials to teach others. He'd sure get the message across about helping one another. And about taking care of the earth's resources. But, first of all, he'd see to it that there would be wilderness areas set aside for wild animals.

He gave a deep sigh of satisfaction and settled back in his seat. Yes, there was something he could do about the world to make it a better place.

Leaving the turnaround, they started up the winding trail which led to the cabin. The snow-covered mountain sparkling in the morning sunlight came into full view. Tom audibly caught his breath. It was the most beautiful sight he'd ever seen.

His grandfather smiled at Tom's reaction. "And I own it all," he said. "I and the Swalalahist, and you and your mother and Julie. And"—his voice, softened—"your father, too, if he ever returns."

"He just might," said Tom. "Mama has always been sure he'll come back." Then, for the first time, it came to him that his father must have a miserable, lonely life. How awful to have to keep moving. What a lot he was missing.

A family—which now included Grandfather. And a home—a whole mountain for a home. And the Swalalahist besides. "Everything is so neat," he said aloud. It was then he noticed the slight frown on his grandfather's face. "Don't you think so?"

"Yes, I suppose it is. I just wonder if your mother will leave when she sees the Swalalahist."

Now Tom laughed. "You don't know Mom. She loves everyone and everything. When she sees the Swalalahist she'll love them too. She'll consider them family. And family is more important to her than anything else."

"What about Julie?"

Tom thought of his blonde, dark-eyed little sister. She had a fierce streak of loyalty. She had Grandfather's mother's blood running in her veins. "No problem," he said, knowing it was so.

They rode along in companionable silence all

the way to the gate. But when Tom began to open the jeep door to get out, his grandfather laid a restraining hand on his arm. "Wait," said the old man. "I have a question to ask."

Dark eyes met dark eyes. "You don't have to ask the question," said Tom. "I guess I've had the answer from the first. Yes, I'll take over the Swalalahist trust." His grin came and went. "And I'll be expecting quite a bit of help."

The old man's grip tightened on his arm and then let go. "Thank you, Tom," he said simply.

When Tom glanced at his grandfather he saw for the second time tears furrowing their way down the leathery cheeks.

Mom did not disappoint him. She accepted the invitation to move to Spirit Mountain with joy and gratitude. "It will be so wonderful to be together as a family, Father," she wrote, "and have a permanent home."

The old man's joy was tempered with anxiety. "I hope this place doesn't seem gloomy to your mother," he said.

"It won't," Tom answered smugly. Grandfather doesn't know it yet, he thought to himself, but wherever Mom goes there is sunshine.

155

In the next few weeks whenever the Swalalahist screamed outside the gate at night, Tom got up too. Together, Grandfather and he would spend an hour or more playing with the big animals.

The Swalalahist, Mr. Buche told him, were mostly night creatures. Tom also found out why the animals clustered around the cabin when it thundered. They were terribly afraid of lightning, and they came to his grandfather for protection.

Tom, whenever possible, accompanied Mr. Buche to the cave. The Swalalahist were always overjoyed to see them. The smallest were permitted to ride in the jeep while the others, chattering and screaming, would run beside the car. Tom and his grandfather sometimes laughed so hard at their antics that tears ran down their faces.

Several times they brought the Swalalahist food—deer meat or gallon jars of Tilly's milk. "No cooked food," the old man instructed Tom. "They are healthy as they are."

But on the second of May when they drove to the cave, no Swalalahist ran to meet them. The cave was empty.

"They are gone," said Grandfather. "Gone back into the mountains for the summer. They're safe there. Hundreds of square miles of wilds where no man has ever set foot. At first frost they'll return."

"I sure will miss them," Tom said. He realized then he had become as attached to the Swalalahist as his grandfather was—and as his grandfather's parents had been—and as all the other Indians who had lived on Spirit Mountain before him. He felt lonely, standing in the silent cave.

But in three weeks Mom and Julie would come. He had so much to tell them. . . .

ABOUT THE AUTHOR

Helen Kronberg Olson, a descendant of one of the earliest Oregon pioneer families, was born and raised in Oregon's Willamette Valley. She was graduated from Mount Angel Women's College with a degree in education. After teaching for several years, she returned to school herself, and later worked for Marion County Welfare, first in the Aid to Dependent Children program and then as a child welfare worker. She was also a social worker for Oregon State Hospital.

Mrs. Olson's hobbies are reading, hiking, and fishing, as well as writing. She has been published extensively in anthologies, magazines, and educational publications, and is the author of a mystery serial. This is her second book.

The mother of one son, Paul, Mrs. Olson and her husband, Harold, live on forty-three acres in the scenic Cascade foothills, where they engage in tree farming. Their home is a cedar house they built themselves.

ABOUT THE ARTIST

Hameed Benjamin was born in New York City and was graduated from the High School of Art and Design in 1965. Later he attended Paine College in Georgia. Noted particularly for the surrealistic treatment of current themes as well as sensitive character inter-pretation, his work has been exhibited in the New York Metropolitan area and in Canada. He resides in New York City with his wife, Kay Brown, who is also an artist.